CHOSEN

CANTERWOOD CREST

CHOSEN

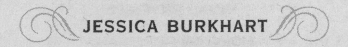
JESSICA BURKHART

ALADDIN MIX

New York London Toronto Sydney

ALADDIN M!X

Simon & Schuster Children's Publishing Division

1230 Avenue of the Americas, New York, NY 10020

First Aladdin M!X edition May 2011

Copyright © 2011 by Jessica Burkhart

All rights reserved, including the right of reproduction

in whole or in part in any form.

ALADDIN is a trademark of Simon & Schuster, Inc., and related logo

is a registered trademark of Simon & Schuster, Inc.

ALADDIN M!X and related logo are registered trademarks

of Simon & Schuster, Inc.

For information about special discounts for bulk purchases, please

contact Simon & Schuster Special Sales at 1-866-506-1949

or business@simonandschuster.com.

The Simon & Schuster Speakers Bureau can bring authors to your live event.

For more information or to book an event contact the Simon & Schuster Speakers

Bureau at 1-866-248-3049 or visit our website at www.simonspeakers.com.

Designed by Mike Rosamilia

The text of this book was set in Venetian 301 BT.

Manufactured in the United States of America 0411 OFF

2 4 6 8 10 9 7 5 3 1

Library of Congress Control Number 2010940033

ISBN 978-1-4424-1946-9

ISBN 978-1-4424-1497-6 (eBook)

To May 2011 being the complete opposite of May 2010.

ACKNOWLEDGMENTS

There wouldn't be a super special without the super team at Simon & Schuster, including Bethany Buck, Fiona Simpson, Mara Anastas, Liesa Abrams, Jessica Handelman, Lucille Rettino, Venessa Williams, Alyson Heller, Russell Gordon, Katherine Devendorf, Karin Paprocki, Ellen Chan, Dayna Evans, and the super all-star Kate Angelella.

Kate the editor, if there's anyone who got lucky to be "chosen," I am. Your edits and countless hours of work on this book made it as shiny as the gold on the cover. Lauren's favorite color, her obsession with PINK, and her admiration of classic style icons are all influenced by you.

Kate the best friend, you define strength, bravery, and grace. During ten months of unimaginable darkness that would have crippled anyone else, you never wavered. Few people call their best friend their hero, but I do. There's not a second of our friendship that I take for granted. I can't wait to watch more *Pretty Little Liars*, shop for sparkly accessories, and eat Ben & Jerry's with you. LYSSM.

Ross, thank you for all the support and for being excited about this new chapter in Canterwood.

Thank you to the stunning new Canterwood models and to Monica Stevenson for taking such gorgeous photographs.

Writing would be lonely without friends, especially Lauren Barnholdt (Barnhart forever!), Rebecca Leach, Mandy Morgan, and Brianna Ahern.

Sparkles to everyone on Team Canterwood for being so awesome! I'm so grateful to all of you for reading the series and for cheering me on while I work. I read and appreciate every Facebook note, Tweet, e-mail, letter, message board post, and blog comment from you.

Finally, saying thank you to the people, both expected and not, who stuck by my best friend in a crisis isn't enough. Those of you who did are forever changed in my eyes.

WEDNESDAY, NOVEMBER 2ND
RED OAK TRIALS
WASHINGTON, D.C.

THE THRILL AT THE CHANCE OF BEING OVER-
all champion at Red Oaks Trials gripped me. Sure, my
team Double Aces seemed to already have cinched the win
for our stable.

But I wanted that individual blue ribbon.

Before cross-country, which was the very last round, I
said as much to my coach.

"I'm going for it," I announced.

"Lauren, I know how driven you are to win," Mr. Wells
said. "But you need to take your time this round. You're
exhausted. If you push it too hard, you're bound to make
a mistake."

"I won't," I insisted. "I studied every jump in this
course when I walked it earlier."

I was cocky—sure I knew better than Mr. Wells. I knew that if I just pushed myself a *tiny* bit further, I could do it. I could.

I mounted Skyblue, the school horse I rode at Aces. Skyblue, a dapple gray gelding, was an experienced competitor. I loved riding him from the day Mr. Wells had paired us together. Skyblue was everything I loved about horses—he was affectionate, calm but fiery when he needed to be, and he listened to his rider.

When the announcer called my name, I entered the starting box. The bell sounded; Skyblue and I were off.

I kept him to a hand gallop as we made our way across the lawn and toward the first jump—a log pile.

On the cross-country course, Skyblue and I raced over several jumps. When I checked my watch, I saw how great our time was. We were so far ahead I could even slow him to a canter, and as long as we stayed on course and didn't have any refusals or problems, we'd win the class.

But I only slowed Skyblue a notch—barely to a canter. He flew down a creek bank, raced though the knee-high water, and his shoes scraped against the creek bed. He scrambled up the embankment and leaped over a fallen tree.

Skyblue didn't question me once.

By the time we reached the end of the woods and hit

the field, I could see them; only two jumps stood between us and the finish line.

Exhilarated, I let Skyblue back into a near gallop as we headed across the meadow toward a brush fence. Wind whooshed in my ears. The chilly air felt good on my face. Skyblue, sweaty but by no means overheated, took fast but even breaths. I looked past the brush at the final jump—a vertical.

Our time is perfect—we've got this! The crowd began cheering as we closed in on the finish line. I never tired of hearing that sound.

Skyblue and I were mere strides away from the brush.

I counted down in my head, preparing to lift out of the saddle and take as much weight off his back as possible.

Almost there. In five, four, three, two—

I never got to one.

Skyblue dug his heels into the grass and skidded to a halt just before the greenery. He was probably close enough that his muzzle brushed the scratchy branches and leaves.

I never saw for sure—I'd flown over the jump without him.

I was unprepared for the refusal. Skyblue had stayed on one side and I'd flown over his head. My entire body slammed into the ground on the other side of the jump. My back hit first, then I rolled onto my shoulder, my helmet thudding against the ground.

I heard a rush of sounds. Of people screaming for help, someone shouting, "Don't move her!" and finally, the ambulance sirens.

"Is Skyblue okay?" I managed to get out. "Is he all right?"

"He's okay, Lauren," Mr. Wells's voice had sounded so off. Shaky. Like he was scared of something.

"Please be still, miss," said someone whose voice I didn't recognize.

I blinked. Mom and Dad knelt beside me, strange expressions on their faces.

Why does everyone look so terrified? I wondered.

Everything went black.

EIGHTEEN MONTHS LATER
UNION, CONNECTICUT

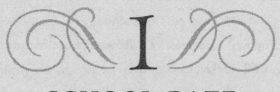

I

SCHOOL DAZE

ON SUNNY MONDAY MORNING, DAD DROVE ME the half hour it took to get to school like he did every morning. He always ended the ride with a funny, "hip" saying. This May morning hadn't been any different.

"G2G, Laur," Dad said. I could see him focus on the acronyms. "Holler back if you need a ride."

Grinning, I got out of the car. "Don't talk to anyone. Please."

Dad headed for work and I went into the school's main building.

I walked down the hallway of Yates Preparatory School to my locker. I dropped my heavy backpack on the floor and spun the combination into my lock until it clicked open. Yates was my fave school so far of all the schools I'd attended. I'd moved around a lot to compete on the show circuit and Yates was my third school.

Doing well academically had always been important to me, and I'd worked hard to keep up my grades while riding. I'd even taken extra courses online last summer. It had paid off when I'd been accepted to Yates.

"Hey, LT."

I peered around the metal door and saw Taylor grinning at me.

"Hi," I said, hugging him. He was a few inches taller than me and his cropped blond hair had been bleached by the sun from spending so many hours practicing in the pool. His tanned skin contrasted with my own pale coloring. I took in the sprinkle of freckles across his nose that I loved.

"Missed you this weekend," I said.

"Me too." Taylor held my hand, leaning up against the lockers. "I hate it when things get so crazy. But Dad insisted that I shadow him at his office, even though it was a weekend."

I rolled my eyes. Taylor and I had been together for five months, and his dad, an investment banker, seemed to want Taylor to decide to follow in the family footsteps and take over the business. Like, yesterday.

"I'm sorry he's pressuring you so much," I said. "We're *twelve*. Aren't we supposed to be able to change whatever we want to be every day if we want?"

Taylor squeezed my hand, letting it go so he could shove his hands into his pockets. "I'm used to it." He smiled. "Anyway, Mondays are gross enough. Let's talk about something waaay better."

"Like?" The enthusiasm in his hazel eyes was infectious.

"Want to go out on Saturday night? We can do something fun—whatever you want."

"Whatever *I* want? I like the sound of that." We smiled at each other. "I'd love to."

The warning bell rang, startling us both. I hadn't even gathered my books for class. Yates had a zero-tolerance policy for lateness and I didn't want to spend my afternoon in detention.

"Perfect," Taylor said. "Text you later."

"Bye."

My excitement about going out with Taylor on Friday made me grab my math book instead of the one I needed for history class. I realized it just before I closed my locker. I switched out the books then hurried to the class I shared with Brielle and Ana.

Yates was so small I got to share a lot of classes with my

two best friends. Everyone knew everyone here. At first, I'd been worried about fitting in. The size of the school made it seem cliquey. But Brielle and Ana had become instant besties.

I snagged a seat in the center of the classroom.

"Hey, Lauren," Amber said, walking inside with her group of friends.

I said hi to her and a few other people as they sat down, furiously opening their textbooks and notebooks. We all wanted to look as if we'd been in class way early to win points with Mr. Newton—one of the toughest teachers at Yates.

"Laur, omigodwehavetotalkrightnow!"

I laughed, looking up at Brielle as she plopped down next to me. Ana sat on my other side, a smile turning up her lips. They were both fun friends to hang out with at school *and* at the stable.

"What's up?" I asked.

Brielle's cool black hair was pulled into a high, shiny ponytail. The gloss treatment we'd all gotten at the salon a couple of weeks ago made her hair look extra gorge. Her fair, freckle-free, never-left-the-house-without-SPF-fifty complexion showed just enough makeup to not get her in trouble with her parents. She had a light coat of mascara, blush, and pale pink-tinted gloss. Brielle was the epitome of a girly-girl.

She looked seasonably adorable today in a Marc Jacobs light pink dress with capped sleeves and a cream-colored cardigan. She had strappy, white wedges to match that I noted (since we were the same shoe size) I'd probably be asking to borrow next week.

"I heard from Kendra, who heard from Madison, who heard from Portia, that Will is going to ask me to the end-of-the-year dance!" Brielle's tone had reached a near shriek.

"That's awesome!" I said, beaming for her.

Ana leaned over toward my desk. "Now we just have to get Will to ask Brielle already, so she can start dress shopping. Even though the dance isn't for a couple of weeks, she's already freaking out about her dress *and* shoes *and* accessories."

"We'll get all of that," I said, glancing between both of my friends. "Taylor's taking me and I haven't picked out anything yet either."

I grinned at Ana in a teasing way. "And are we getting *you* into a dress?"

"No!" Ana groaned. "Isn't it enough that I'm going? I'm happy you both have dates, and I'm going to be there from the hair blow-out to the fastening of your strappy shoes, but I'm going solo. You know I'm only focused on two things—"

Brielle and I finished the sentence along with her. "Writing and illustrating."

Ana pulled out her notebook that she'd covered in gorgeous pen sketches of people, animals, buildings, and anything else that had caught her attention.

"I'm an *artiste*," Ana said, her tone playful. "I refuse to be distracted by boys. Or anything else."

Brielle and I didn't argue with her. Ana was one of the most talented artists at our entire school. She dressed the part, too. Today, she was *très* (French for "very") chic in an ivory beret that was slightly back behind her hairline, black leggings, and ballet flats. She'd curled her light brown hair into waves and the highlights made her skin tone glow.

She pushed the makeup rule a little more than Brielle. She'd been doing it for months and had never gotten in trouble. This morning she had a thin line of black liquid eyeliner with the slightest cat-eye curve that looked amazing and brought out her wide, brown eyes.

"Speaking of which, is your creative writing group today?" I asked Ana.

"Yeah, I'm meeting up with art class friends to critique one another's sketches. It's one of our last meetings before school's out for summer. You guys?"

"I'm doing nothing for finals," Brielle said. "Boring."

"I've got glee club," I said. "Then homework for me."

"Glee will be distracting," Ana said. "Hopefully it'll keep you from thinking about Canterwood."

Canterwood Crest Academy—those three words made my skin prickle. Canterwood was one of the best, most prestigious boarding schools in the country with an extremely well-known riding program. From what I'd heard, the extracurriculars there—in particular the equestrian team—were as tough as the academics.

Ever since I'd heard about it, I'd been obsessed with Canterwood. I loved everything about the school—from its green and gold school colors to the photos on the Web site to the descriptions of the student dorms.

I'd applied months ago and once I started thinking about it, I couldn't stop. I was already close to camping out in front of my mailbox.

"Definitely," I said, smiling. "I'm just ready to get through classes and go to glee."

Glee club was one of the only things that made me look forward to Mondays. I wasn't even close to being the best singer in the club, but I loved singing and performing. Last week our club had performed a new song from Sierra, a hot new hip-hop artist, and it had been so much fun. Our club just formed this year and we were already prepping to start competing next year.

Next year.

Next year I'd likely be at Yates competing in glee. Or maybe, just maybe, I'd be competing somewhere different altogether. Somewhere like Canterwood Crest Academy.

2

FROM THE TOP

"LET'S TAKE IT FROM THE TOP," MR. BENSON said. "The last run-through was great and I can tell you've all been practicing. But I want to hear it again. This time, with a little more *energy*."

The twelve of us nodded from our chairs in the school's music room. I *loved* it in here. The glossy wooden floors looked even shinier from the sunlight that poured through two tall windows in the back. Musical notes, painted in black and silver, kept the white walls from looking plain and institutional. A set of red Yamaha drums were in the far corner and in the back of the room, a baby grand piano made me wish I knew how to play.

Mr. Benson, one of the youngest teachers, had a reputation for being cool because he let us mix up contemporary music with the older music most glee club teachers taught. He'd also installed a killer sound system in our room so when we sang, the acoustics were just right.

Glee club was the first club I'd joined.

Ever.

At my old schools, I'd always been too busy with riding. It had been my *only* priority. Riding was still my primary focus, but I'd always secretly wanted to sing and perform. My first day at Yates, I'd noticed an audition sheet by the guidance counselor's office. I walked past the sheet at least six times before I'd finally scribbled *Lauren Towers* on the paper, below dozens of other names. The chance to be part of an activity that depended solely on me and not a thousand-pound animal had sounded so exciting—so different. Riding had always been a fifty-fifty thing—part of my performance depended on me and the other part was up to my horse. But with something like glee club, whether I sang well or not, was all in my control.

I'd auditioned for Mr. Benson, singing a few lines from one of my favorite songs—"Begin Again."

Mr. Benson had thanked me politely—he hadn't given the tiniest hint if I'd made it or not. He just told all of the people who'd auditioned to come back the next day after class. Then he'd told us we'd all done a wonderful job and that if he called our name, we'd made it. When Mr. Benson called my name, I'd almost fallen off the stage. The girl who'd thought she was only good at one thing—and maybe not even that—had been chosen for glee club! To sing and dance in the spotlight. I'd been ecstatic.

Now Mr. Benson sat in front of the piano, his fingers flying over the keys. I reminded myself to stay focused on *energy* and when we started singing, Jared started clapping and got the whole group's energy up. I was grateful.

Jared, our glee club leader, always gave extra energy to the group even on the longest, gloomiest days. He was so friendly and he always gave advice to anyone who needed it—he wasn't a solo hog. Jared wanted our entire club to do well and he never acted like he had the best voice, even though he did. He could sing anything—his range was incredible.

Our voices did that magic thing where they all just seemed to melt together, and when we finished the song, we fell silent, looking to Mr. Benson for his opinion. But even before his face broke into a smile, we all knew we'd nailed it—thanks to Jared.

"That's *exactly* what I was hoping to hear, guys," Mr. Benson said. He bowed his head to us, slapping a palm on top of the piano with excitement. "As long as you keep practicing on your own over the summer, we'll be ready to start competing in the fall. We'll keep in touch via a locked glee club message board that I've been working on. We have something to discuss already: It's time to decide on a name for our club."

"Cool!" Jared said. "It's about time we got a name."

I smiled along with Jared and everyone else, but part of my happy look was fake. I loved the club and I'd been a member all year, but would I be here when we got a name? Or when we started competing? My feelings about Canterwood versus Yates changed daily. One day, all I wanted was to be a student at what looked like my dream school. The next, I wanted to stay where I felt comfortable—where I fit in and had friends and was even *popular*.

A place I could excel even if . . . even if I could never jump again. I loved riding, but I didn't know if going back to a life of equestrian competition was what I wanted. Sometimes, I thought it was. Other times, I wanted everyone to forget that I was a "good" dressage rider and I thought I'd be happy just pleasure riding Cricket from now on.

Would the right decision be to start all over *again* and risk everything at a brand new school? Was it wrong if I started feeling comfortable enough at Yates to be just another normal student—one who studied hard and got good grades and did nothing but safe, fun glee club after school? No one shouting at me about confidence, or moving past bad memories. Would it be so wrong to be part of an ensemble for once rather than to ride solo?

You're getting ahead of yourself. You don't even know if you got in. So stop obsessing until you get an answer—which will very, VERY likely be thanks, but no thanks.

But when I got home, I couldn't help myself—I walked over to the wire mail bin where whoever checked the mail placed it for everyone else to look through. Dad's mail was already gone and Becca had a card from Gram in a bright orange envelope.

Nothing for me.

I stared at the basket for a while—not sure if I was disappointed or kind of glad that there was nothing from Canterwood.

3

DESIGNER BOOTS
TO FILL

THE FINAL VERTICAL LOOMED IN FRONT OF me during Wednesday's group riding lesson. It looked higher than any jump I'd ever attempted. Sure, I'd cleared fences higher than the approaching blue rails before. But ever since I'd applied to Canterwood Crest Academy months ago, the jumps—and the stakes—had gotten higher.

"Lauren!" Kim, my riding instructor, called across the outdoor arena. "Tighten your reins and slow Cricket. She's trying to rush the last jump."

Come on, I told myself. *You're supposed to be Lauren Towers. You should be able to do this stuff.*

I pushed my weight into the saddle to signal the Welsh-Cob pony mix to slow. Jumping wasn't *my* strongest area, but it was Cricket's. The school horse, sweet and, more important, smart, knew just when to try and catch me off guard.

Cricket hesitated, almost as if trying to decide whether or not to listen. She could be a little hard to handle sometimes, but that had been Kim's intention when I'd come to Briar Creek. She'd wanted to challenge me by giving me Cricket to ride. I'd disagreed at first, especially after . . . *no, NOT thinking about that now.* I shut the memory out of my brain and tried to focus on my ride.

Cricket's small hooves churned up the arena dirt and she tossed her head, not wanting to slow. I did a half-halt, but Cricket surged ahead. Panic rippled in my stomach.

It didn't help that a group of students gathered along the fence, watching my ride. At the opposite end of the arena, I spotted Ana, offering me silent support. Brielle hadn't been able to make it today because she had to babysit.

In my head, I could hear Ana yelling at me, telling me these were the basics and I should have this. There was no excuse—I was making beginner mistakes.

"Lauren! Get Cricket's attention!" Kim shouted.

I could feel my face getting red. Everyone's eyes were on me and the last thing I wanted was to mess up in front of them.

We were strides away from the jump and I was too nervous to relax. In my mind, the handful of people watching turned into a crowd and they were judging my ride. The jump rushed toward us at a dizzying pace and fear took over. Spots swam in front of my eyes. This was almost like *before*.

I yanked Cricket's right rein, turning her away from the jump. The sudden sideways movement almost tossed me out of the saddle. Frustrated, Cricket threw her head in the air and half-bucked as I cantered her *far* away from the jump. I gripped as hard as I could with my knees, fighting to stay on.

I slowed her to a trot and, finally, a walk. My heartbeat seemed to slow the farther away from the jump we got.

"Lauren," Kim said my name again. She walked over to Cricket and me. "You okay?"

"I'm fine," I said. "I'm sorry. I—I couldn't do it."

I didn't look at anyone who was watching. But I was sure they were all whispering about what had happened. That was one of the worst performances I'd had in a long time. I was supposed to be *the* Lauren Towers. Now everyone probably thought I was a joke.

"Everyone else is finished, so I'd like you to cool and groom Cricket, then come by my office. Okay?" Kim asked.

I nodded.

Kim touched my shoulder, then turned to address the other riders. But I didn't hear her. It was like a silent movie. Everyone dismounted and started toward the stable. I watched Ana hand her horse to one of the girls who'd been watching and then make her way toward me.

I dismounted, patting Cricket's neck.

"We'll get it next time, girl. Promise," I said. We'd jumped a million times before—I had to keep reminding myself of that. But it wasn't easy.

I took off my helmet. The warm May air had made my long, dark brown hair stick to my forehead. I let my hair down and then gathered the natural waves into a ponytail. Afterward, I loosened Cricket's girth and started to lead her in a circle.

"Is everything okay?" Ana asked, reaching me. Her eyes were wide with worry.

"I was so ridiculous," I said. "Cricket was set to jump and I stopped her. I . . . got scared."

"That's okay," Ana said. "You have every right to be nervous about jumping." She ran her fingers through her light brown hair. "But what matters is that you don't beat yourself up and that you remember you *have* done this before. And really well!"

"Everyone's probably in the stable laughing at me," I said.

"No, they're not," Ana said firmly. "Don't worry about that. Next time you jump, you're going to *fly* over it without a problem. I know it."

I smiled a little. Ana had been one of my biggest cheerleaders since I'd started at Briar Creek.

"I'll be ready next time," I said. I tried to make sure what I said sounded like a statement and not a question.

Ana nodded. "You so will be."

Ana stayed with me for a few more minutes before her mom came to pick her up. Before she'd left, Ana had switched the subject to the weird mystery smell in homeroom. She'd made me laugh and I'd gotten past my bad ride with Ana's help. I *had* conquered a lot of jumps since my accident, and just because I hadn't today didn't mean I was a failure.

I walked Cricket out of the arena and past the wooden fence boards that had been painted a light brown last month. Kim had been busy making all kinds of repairs to the only riding stable in town.

I hadn't been living in Union, Connecticut long, but since I'd been here, Briar Creek had become my oasis. It had given me what I'd needed—an escape and time off from competition. It had also taught me how to *really* love horses again.

Kim had played a huge role in the way I felt about Briar Creek. She was one of the best instructors I'd ever had. The most exciting part about Kim was that she'd taught the stable's star, Sasha Silver, all she'd needed to know to leave Briar Creek and get into Canterwood Crest Academy.

Kim, familiar with the process because of Sasha, had helped me with my application. I'd sent transcripts from Yates, a DVD I'd made of myself riding, and two letters of recommendation—one from Kim and the other from my French II teacher.

I asked Kim to tell me everything she knew about the equestrian team at Canterwood. Kim told me everything, especially about how tough the instructor, Mr. Conner, was on his students.

The biggest shock had been when Kim told me that I'd been here when Sasha had come to visit one day. Sasha Silver had been on the grounds and I hadn't even known it. I wondered if she'd seen me.

That's why I'd been checking the mailbox every day since January fourth. Every day since I'd applied to Canterwood Crest.

Briar Creek was so different from Canterwood. Kim

was the only instructor here and there were riders of every level and age. A few adult riders schooled young horses in the metal, orange round pens that Kim had spaced out on the grassy sides of the drive.

A college-age girl smiled down at me from her black-and-white Appaloosa as she headed out for the trails. That's where I wished I was going—anywhere but Kim's office to talk.

It couldn't be good and my gut felt knotted. Maybe Kim wanted to take back her recommendation letter.

I untacked, groomed, fed, and watered Cricket, then led her into her stall. She took a dainty sip of water before turning around in the deep sawdust to grab a bite of hay.

Reluctant to leave her, I walked down the quiet aisle to Kim's office. I wished that Ana or Brielle could come in with me. I reached Kim's office and tapped my fingers against her half-open door.

"Come in," she said.

I smiled as best I could and sat in the chair across from her. Behind Kim, photos and paintings of her beloved horses covered the reddish-brown walls. Her tiny office had a cluttered desk, an overflowing metal file cabinet, and multicolored ribbons strung along the wall. There was a shelf of trophies and the biggest one wasn't hard to miss. Its shiny gold gleamed, and the name etched on to the plaque was familiar to everyone here—*Sasha Silver.*

"Lauren, don't look so down," Kim said, smiling at me.

"I'm sorry about the jump," I said. "It's not going to happen every time."

Kim folded her hands into a steeple on her desk. "Of course it's not—you're a good jumper. And I'm not upset with you. But I want to talk to you for a second about something else." She paused. "About Canterwood."

The words sent my heartbeat into overdrive. I nodded.

"As I've said many times before, I believe you're a perfect candidate for the school. But Lauren, I can tell as decision time gets closer that your nerves are affecting your ride."

I lowered my head. She was right.

"We are so privileged to have you here at Briar Creek," Kim said. "It's been an honor to have you as a student. But when I first found out that you were coming, we talked. And you told me you'd come for one reason. . . ."

I swallowed, not wanting to think about it.

Kim stared at me expectantly, waiting for me to continue her thought.

"I came to get away from being Lauren Towers," I said. "The nationally ranked junior dressage champion. I came to learn what loving riding meant again. And I have." I smiled. "You gave me that back."

Kim's happy expression matched mine, but I knew she wanted me to continue. To voice the one thing I'd purposefully left unsaid.

I took a breath. "And . . . I came to get my confidence back after my jumping accident."

Just saying the words was as far as my brain would let me go. I wasn't ready to think about it yet. To relive any of it. Any of the sounds, or smells, or worse than anything, the *feeling*. The total loss of control—the helplessness.

"Confidence that was there all along," Kim said. "Since your family moved to Union, you've done nothing but move forward. You're incredibly talented for most riders—let alone a twelve-year-old."

"Thank you," I said. "But when I think about my application to Canterwood, I get scared all over again."

Kim's smile was gentle. "You know who else was *terrified* when she applied to Canterwood?"

I shook my head. "Who?"

"Sasha," Kim said. "She talked to me almost every day about how scared she was."

"Sasha Silver? Really?" I couldn't believe the superstar rider, only a year older than me, had been nervous about going to Canterwood. I'd watched dozens of DVDs of her shows—Kim had always used her as an example whenever she wanted to encourage my riding class.

"Really. She almost didn't go to Canterwood because she was worried that she wouldn't measure up to the other riders," Kim said.

She glanced up at a picture of Sasha and her horse on the wall. "But she couldn't stay here," Kim continued. "Briar Creek was her home for a little while. But it was really just a bridge to Canterwood. That's what I hope it will be for you. You're ready to compete again, Lauren. The only way to quiet your fears is to face them."

I was still for a moment before I responded. "I guess I'll know in a few weeks if I'm ready or not, huh?"

"Either way," Kim said. "It's time for you to stop worrying and go enjoy the rest of your weekend! Who knows—you may not have many more of them left here."

"You sound so confident, like you're sure I'll get in."

"Your application was strong," Kim said. "Especially your DVD."

"This might be completely out of line," I said. "But did you tell them about my jumping problem?"

Kim nodded. "I did."

Those two words had sealed Canterwood's decision. There was no way I was getting in now.

I held back tears, refusing to cry in Kim's office.

"Lauren," Kim's voice was soft. "I told them you're working past your accident and that you're getting stronger with every jump you take. An experience like you had will make you a stronger applicant in their eyes. You've overcome so much to get where you are."

But I barely heard what Kim said. My application to Canterwood had gone right in the trash—I knew it. And my DVD? The one Kim had said was "strong"? That was a giant fake. I'd practiced and practiced and *practiced* on camera, then had taken the footage home to watch it. I'd chosen the segment of tape where I'd done my absolute best and erased the rest of the footage. There weren't any outtakes to erase at Canterwood.

" . . . so don't think that what you're working through is going to prevent you from being accepted," Kim said when I finally tuned in again. "The instructor will see a talented all-around rider who needs practice—like you're doing every day—to do well at your sport."

I nodded, forcing myself to smile. I didn't want Kim to think I was ungrateful—she was busy enough and she'd taken time to write me a recommendation.

"Thanks, Kim," I said. "You're right. And I better go—my dad's probably waiting."

Kim's lips parted, like she wanted to say something, but she let me go.

Outside the stable, an odd sense of relief came over me. At least I knew for sure what Canterwood's answer was going to be. The only thing I'd be checking the mailbox for now was an official rejection.

In the distance, I watched a chestnut graze. He made me think of Sasha's horse, Charm. *Sasha's going to remain the only Union girl at Canterwood*, I thought. She had left some giant Ariat boots to fill, but I was definitely not going to be doing that at Canterwood.

4

LAUREN TOWERS
KNOWS STYLE

DAD AND I TALKED NONSTOP THE ENTIRE drive home from Briar Creek. I'd kept up the chatter and steered clear of anything Canterwood related. I'd always known in my gut that I wouldn't get in, so the confirmation hadn't been too disappointing. I was glad, even. Right . . . ?

As we pulled into our driveway, Dad reached over and squeezed my hand. His cool blue eyes, the same shade as mine, were steady. I loved that our eyes matched even though he was my stepdad. My real dad had died when I was a just baby and Gregg was the only—and best—dad I'd ever known.

"I know you better than you think, Laur-Bell," Dad said. He put his sunglasses on top of his head. "What's wrong?"

"Nothing," I said. "Totally fine."

Dad glanced at me before putting our black SUV in park and turning off the ignition. "Totally fine, huh? You're sure *nothing's* wrong?" Dad prompted, his tone gentle.

"I was just . . . talking to Kim about Canterwood. I really don't think I'm going to get in, but I knew that already."

Before Dad could continue the conversation, I opened the door, hauled my riding bag out with me, and hopped out. The more I said the school's name, the more I realized I was a little more upset than I'd told myself I was. *But you never counted on being accepted in the first place, so stop it,* I scolded myself. *Focus on something else.*

I looked at our new house as we approached it. We'd moved a few hours north to Union from Brooklyn, and having a house felt massive compared to our old apartment. On the outside, the five-bedroom home was light with dark gray stones all the way from the bottom of the doorway to the white peak of the roof. Near the peak, a window in the attic stared over the lawn. The rest of the house had eggshell-colored siding, and a three-car garage sat off to the right. Along the landing, shrubs flourished in the dark soil that our gardener had just churned up and the leafy greens added a pop of color in front of the gray house. The grass, trimmed low from our lawn service, made the house look tidy and perfect. I followed Dad along our sidewalk, past the small black lampposts that lined either side and up two white-brick stairs to the front door.

Through the gold-etched glass, I could see Mom coming to open the door as Dad fumbled in his pocket for his keys.

"Hi, guys," Mom said, pulling open the door. Her honey-colored hair was back in a skinny gray headband. She had a white V-neck T-shirt over Michael Kors black leggings and, guessing from the pen and papers in her hand, she'd just come out of her home office.

We greeted her as I took off my boots and put them in the coat closet. I pulled off my sweaty socks and dropped them in a laundry basket that was along the wall near the kitchen.

In the kitchen, I realized that Ellen, our housekeeper, must already be here.

"Any mail for me?" I asked, following Mom through the foyer. I wanted the letter, to get it over with.

"Sorry, sweetie. Nothing from Canterwood." She put down the pile of manila folders she'd been carrying on a cherry-wood end table and took my hand. "It's going to come, Lauren. Just have patience. Go shower and I'll make you and Becca a snack. I'll eat with you girls, then I've got to get back to my office to read a few legal briefs."

Mom's office was off to the side of the library. It was filled with case files and documents I couldn't even try to understand. She was a partner at the biggest law firm outside of Union and that meant she was *always* working. Dad said I got my drive to work hard at riding from my mother.

I left the foyer and started up the spiral staircase, my hand gliding on the dark wooden rail. My bare feet sank into the plush beige carpet as I crept to Becca's room.

"Hey," I said, pausing in her doorway. There was a red-and-white polka dot swimsuit on her bed.

"You have a good lesson?" she asked.

Beautiful, blond Becca was two years older than me and we had a relationship all of my friends envied—we were sisters and best friends.

"It wasn't the best."

"Sorry," Becca said. "I'm sure the next one will be better."

Becca, sitting on her dark purple comforter, motioned for me to come into her room. She had a night table on either side of her bed, each of which held piles of brightly colored books and clear lamps with plum shades. Her room was a fun mix of deep purple and white—from the cloud-white shag rug in front of her bed to the flowy, purple velvet curtains over the windows.

"You still look down," Becca said. "I know what this is about, Laur."

My sister knew me too well.

"I couldn't jump," I said. "And Kim told Canterwood that."

"What? No," Becca said. "What are you talking about?"

I told Becca what Kim had told me.

"Laur, Kim did the right thing," Becca said. "She told them that Lauren Towers is a rider who's working on overcoming her fears. A rider who didn't give up and one who wants to get into a school where she'll be challenged."

Becca smiled, shaking her head at me. "You're *so* getting in. I should start helping you pack now."

"There's no way," I argued. "They'll see me as a failure. The girl who had an accident and is still afraid a year and a half later."

"Okay, so they'll think you're scared. But you're scared *and* jumping anyway."

I looked at Becca—the sister who'd never lied to me

and who always made me feel better. For some crazy reason, I almost believed her.

Almost.

"I mean, c'mon," Becca said, her tone light. "When have *I* ever been wrong?"

Her Cheshire Cat grin made me smile—I couldn't help it. "Oh, please," I said, rolling my eyes and laughing.

"When you get in, I'll be right—again. Like always. So I'd start hoping again that you see the acceptance letter soon," Becca said.

I didn't know if I wanted to shake Becca or hug her. She'd just raised my hopes. A *teensy* bit. A microscopic bit.

"I guess this is the one time I really want you to be right," I said. "So, I guess we'll have to wait and see."

"Good. In the meantime, you've got *plenty* of things to do—starting with hanging out with me in the pool after we eat."

I smiled, knowing what she was doing but letting her.

"I turned up the heater in the pool so it's not so chilly," Becca said. "I know Mom's making snacks, so I'm going to eat and then work on my tan for a while. I so need someone out there or I'll be bored."

"I guess I can help with that," I teased. "And my muscles are sore from riding."

Becca's cell phone rang and she reached over to answer it. I could tell just by the look on her face that it was her boyfriend, Grant.

I left her room and went into my own, tossing my riding clothes in the hamper and then shutting myself in my bathroom. My color scheme was very different from Becca's. I liked softer shades and things with a delicate, classic style. My bathroom matched my bedroom—light blue and white towels, alternating in color, hung clean and fluffy on the towel rack, and the blue shower curtain with white pinstripes pulled the entire look together. Style was important to me. My fashion icons were Audrey Hepburn and Jacqueline Kennedy Onassis—two beautiful women who embraced classic American style with clean lines and gorgeous, ornate accessories, such as a pair of oversized sunglasses or a single strand of pearls.

After my shower, I changed into a red bandeau top and bikini bottoms. I threw on a white oversized tissue T-shirt and headed down to eat.

Becca, already seated at the kitchen island, had a violet Pottery Barn pool towel wrapped around her shoulders. Mom put a plate in front of each of us.

"Thanks, Mom," Becca and I said.

Mom had put out a side of applesauce and tiny

single-serving cartons of ice cream. That's where Becca and I differed—she was a chocolate freak and I wasn't. Phish Food for her and Dulce de Leche for me.

We ate our snacks together, and then headed through the living room and out the sliding glass doors to a maple-stained wooden deck. I tossed my towel on one of the five lawn chairs, the wooden planks warm under my feet. Off to the side, Dad's massive—like, ridiculously huge—grill was along the wall near the door to the sauna.

Becca and I went to the pool closet and looked for our rafts—one purple and one blue. Mom and Dad's matching red rafts were off to the side with Charlotte's. My older sister had left last fall to attend college at Sarah Lawrence in Bronxville, New York—outside of New York City. I missed her, but there had always been a rivalry between us. I was the athlete, the rider who *had* to be number one, and she was the overachiever who studied until two a.m., was in every imaginable club, and *also* had to be number one.

I tossed my raft into the clear water, causing ripples. Holding on to the railing, I dipped a French-manicured toe into the perfect stillness that eventually settled around the raft.

"It's *amazing*," I said. "The water feels sooo good."

Becca started down the stairs, wading into the

shallow end of the pool, swirling her fingers in the water. I walked alongside the pool to the opposite end and stepped onto the diving board, balancing with my arms out as I reached the end and sat down, dangling my legs. It felt good to be out here—away from the stable and everything related to riding and Canterwood. Plus, Becca was an expert at keeping my mind off things I didn't want to think about.

Becca, now situated on her raft, put on her sunglasses and glanced over at me.

"It's weird to see you out here," she said. "But I'm glad you're here."

"*Weird*? Why?" Playfully, I kicked a bit of water in her direction.

"Lauren!" She half-sat up on her elbow, looking at me. "I'll come up there and push you off the diving board."

I stuck my tongue out at my older sister. "Answer my question. What's weird about me being in the pool?"

Becca skimmed her fingertips across the top of the water. "I'm just not used to seeing you so . . . relaxed," she said. "You're always either at the stable or obsessing over shows. But after the . . . " She stopped, chewing on her bottom lip. "Sorry."

"No, it's okay." I realized I was making the diving

board shake with my dangling feet. "I have to start talking about it sometime. It was a long time ago."

"You don't have to talk about it. We came out here to chill."

I stood up, balancing on my toes at the edge of the board. "You know, you're right."

Without another word, I bounced up and down on the board, arching my back, then pushing off with my feet and diving into the water.

I kicked to the bottom of the deep end and touched my fingertips to the pool floor. For a few seconds, I stayed down longer than I needed. I wished the cool water could make every memory, every detail of that day vanish. But absolutely nothing could erase it.

When my lungs began to burn as if they were going to burst, I pushed up and I sucked in huge breaths as I broke the water's surface. I wiped the water out of my eyes and swam over to my raft, ignoring the *I'm-your-big-sister-and-I-know-you're-thinking-about-it* look from Becca.

"What's Taylor doing this weekend?" Becca asked. She knew I could talk about my boyfriend for hours.

"He's busy," I said. "But we're going out on Friday."

"At least your boyfriend goes to your school," Becca said. "Grant has swim practice today *and* his stepwitch is dragging him to a fancy polo match on Saturday that'll be filled with olds and snobs."

I shot her an apologetic glance. "But you guys must have plans for next week, right?"

"Wednesday night," Becca confirmed. "We're doing homework at his house and after, we're going to see a movie."

"Cool. That'll be fun."

Becca kept me talking as we floated in the pool. The more we talked, the more hopeful I felt—about my jumping skills and Canterwood. Talking about Taylor and my friends made me happy and, for the rest of the afternoon, not a single memory about my accident resurfaced.

5

GROOM AND
GOSSIP

AFTER SCHOOL, I HURRIED UP BRIAR CREEK'S gravel driveway eager to get my lesson over with and go on a leisurely trail ride that Brielle and Ana and I had planned for after our session. We deserved it after a crazy week at school.

I spotted Cricket grazing in the pasture with a few of Kim's school horses. Some of the fences had noticeable cribbing marks. Kim had been talking for months about how she'd get the boards replaced soon, but I liked them the way they were. It made me feel comfortable—unlike some of the chi-chi stables I'd been to before. They'd felt like a fancy house where everyone was afraid to sit on the couches or touch anything that looked as if it would cost a zillion dollars to replace.

I knew how lucky I was to have grown up like I did. My parents had always done well and provided me with whatever I needed. Competing and traveling wasn't inexpensive and Mom and Dad had made sure I'd pitched in. I'd always groomed my own horse, cleaned stalls, and done stable chores, unlike many of my competitors. The girls who'd worked their horses to a sweat and passed them off to waiting groom had never been my friends. They thought having money made them better than everyone else, but really, it just made them people I never wanted to call friends.

I brought my bag of riding clothes into the tiny bathroom and closed the wooden door behind me, sliding the lock shut. The orange walls had tiny cracks near the ceiling, but everything was spotless. My phone chimed as I finished zipping up my heather gray Mossimo hoodie over my favorite PINK brand T-shirt—black with a red metallic heart and silver stitching. My parents had just started to let me shop the Victoria's Secret PINK clothing and pajama line last year, and I spent almost every cent of my allowance there. The whole collection was bright and colorful with pretty, delicate designs adorned with sprays of glitter and sometimes even tiny sequins that made you look *très*-glam even in loungey clothes. If Audrey Hepburn were alive today, I'd bet she'd shop PINK all the time. There was something to be said for sparkling even while you slept. I was so into PINK, I even followed them on Chatter.

I grabbed my BlackBerry from my purse and opened BlackBerry messenger.

Ana:

Brielle & I r 10 mins away. U there yet?

I typed a message back.

Lauren:

Here! Grabbing Cricket from pasture & going 2 outdoor arena 2 practice. C u there.

Before I put away my phone, I typed a quick Chatter update: *Abt 2 ride w @AnaArtiste & @BrielleisaBeauty. Hoping 2day's lesson goes well! 4:28 p.m.*

I got a Chat back from Ana immediately. *@LaurBell* ☺ *4:29 p.m.*

I finished packing my school clothes into my bag and took it to my cubby in the room where students kept their stuff. Nothing had locks because we didn't need them. At my last stable, security was so tight I'd been surprised there hadn't been any armed guards. Every rider had a locked space and there were signs everywhere warning riders that if expensive items like phones, laptops, or iPods went missing, it was the rider—not the stable—that was liable.

I didn't need a lead line to get Cricket, but I did want to take her a treat. I rifled through my tack trunk, took out a few snacks from the Jolly Goodies bag that I'd ordered from State Line Tack, and walked toward the pasture. Treats in hand, I undid the semirusty chain on the metal gate and closed it behind me. Once I was a ways into the pasture, I stopped, letting out the piercing whistle that Cricket knew well.

Her head snapped up from the grass and looked around for me. She spotted me and broke into a trot, leaving the other grazing horses behind. Her hoof beats, muffled by the grass that had been cropped by grazing horses, made me smile. I loved that sound.

Rhythmic. Beautiful. Just like the animal herself. I'd loved everything about horses since I'd ridden my first one at a kindergarten birthday party when I was five. I'd begged-slash-whined about riding until my parents had signed me up for beginner lessons at Winding Road—a tiny stable near our Syracuse home where I'd been born. It was a short drive to the stable since the city in upstate New York wasn't very big.

I rode at Winding Road Stable for years, moving fast

from beginner, to intermediate, to advanced. My instructor, Mr. Scott, entered me in my first show at six, and from then on, I was hooked on competition.

My parents had been hesitant at first to let me compete, but after they saw how much I loved showing, they allowed me to enter a show every few months. That turned into every couple of months, and then every few weeks as I got older. It didn't take long for me to move through local, state, and regional shows. Mr. Scott told my parents that I was ready to compete nationally.

Eventually, I started traveling, mostly with Dad since Mom's job as a lawyer kept her working ten hour days at the office. Dad worked from home as a freelance technical writer, which meant he wrote books and articles. I never could understand those articles—I even secretly thought it must be a pretty boring job, but he always smiled when he worked and the job meant he could accompany me to every show and I never had to travel with a chaperone or nanny like most of my teammates.

When I was eight, Mom got a better job at a bigger law firm in Brooklyn and we'd left Syracuse. Brooklyn had felt like home from the second I'd stepped into our apartment, which I hadn't seen much of since I'd traveled a lot. When we'd moved again, I'd been glad to escape the apartment that I'd had nightmares in for weeks after my accident. I loved Union, but now, when I thought about Brooklyn, I kind of missed it. The fun memories I had from the apartment were slowly starting to overshadow the bad I'd experienced while living there.

Cricket slowed to a walk as she approached me. "Hi, girl," I said. The dainty bay stuck her head toward my outstretched hand, inhaling the scent of apple and cinnamon. She carefully lipped the treats from my hand and I laughed at her chin whiskers tickling my palm.

Union offered an option Brooklyn hadn't—a chance for me to have my *own* horse—something Mom and Dad hadn't caved on yet. I'd wanted one since I'd started riding, but they didn't want me to be spoiled. It had never impacted my riding, thankfully, because I'd been lucky enough to have good school horses to ride. But I was still waiting for the day when Mom and Dad said I'd earned the privilege to have my own horse.

"Time to get you groomed and ready for our lesson," I told her, grasping the light blue halter that made her dark coat look even richer.

I touched a hand to my own face, too, feeling the smile that was ever present whenever I was near a horse. I couldn't stop it even if I tried—and, safe or not—a tiny voice in my head reminded me that nothing, not even glee, made me feel the way I did when I was with a horse I loved.

I led Cricket out of the pasture and toward the stable. Inside, I spotted Ana and Brielle's horses, that were school horses like Cricket, waiting in our usual spot. We always tied the horses together at the end of the stable so we could catch up on school gossip. True, we BBM'd every chance we got during school hours, but there was something about grooming and gossiping in person that was better, even than Häagen Dazs Dulce de Leche ice cream.

"Hey, guys," I said to Ana and Brielle. "You got here fast. And cute shirt." I nodded at Ana's long-sleeved white shirt with a chestnut horse rearing on the back.

"Thanks," Ana sad, smiling. "I found the coolest new store online—Wolf & Harrison. They have the cutest horse-themed stuff."

"We changed at school, BTW," Brielle said, her raven hair still shimmering in a low ponytail. "Our horses were already in their stalls. We looked for you in Cricket's stall, but it was empty, so we figured she was outside."

"Yeah, Kim must have forgotten to bring her in," I said, tying up Cricket. "But it's no big. She won't take long to groom—it looks like she didn't roll in the grass."

"We can watch her while you grab her tack and grooming box," Ana offered.

"Thanks. Be right back."

I quickly grabbed Cricket's English saddle, pad, and bridle from the tiny tack room. The riders who had their own horses kept their tack in trunks outside of their horses' stalls. The stable's tack was kept in the tack room.

I picked up my grooming box—a new one I'd gotten for Christmas last year. It was the nicest one I'd ever had—my favorite shade of blue with glitter specks painted into the plastic finish. I'd also gotten a matching set of brushes, combs, and a pretty hoof pick.

The memory of when I'd opened the grooming kit flashed in my brain. I'd already opened boxes with clothes, books, and fun jewelry, saving the biggest box for last. Mom and Dad had looked so excited for me to open it and I hadn't even been able to conjure a guess as to what it was. When I'd opened it, I'd fought to keep a smile on my face. I *loved* the gift, but it hadn't been that long since my accident. I'd been going back and forth between accepting what had happened and being terrified of horses.

Thankfully, no one had noticed I'd been upset. No one except for Becca. She'd steered conversation away from me and the tack box, but had found me in my room later. Like always, Becca made sure I was okay. She'd invited me into her room and we'd watched *White Christmas* together until I'd fallen asleep.

When I reached Brielle and Ana, we fell into our routine of grooming and gossiping. I watched Brielle brush Zane, the albino gelding she rode. She had to work harder than anyone to keep her horse clean. I loved Zane, but I didn't envy Brielle. The tiniest of grass stains took Mane 'n Tail shampoo to scrub it out. She had to bathe him at least once a week during warm weather.

"I'm sooo glad this school year is almost over," Brielle said. "Being in seventh grade is going to be so cool. We'll be . . ."

Brielle let her arm drop down, clutching the red body brush she'd been using on Zane. Ana shot Brielle a quick look.

"What was that?" I asked, stepping around Cricket so I could see them both.

Brielle glanced at Ana and then back at me. "I, um, didn't mean to start talking about next year. Sorry. Forget I said anything. I don't want to think about it."

I shook my head, genuinely confused. "Why not?"

"Because you might not be here," Brielle said, her brown eyes looking down, then back at me.

Her words caught me *completely* off guard. I actually felt myself take a step back. I couldn't believe she was saying that now, especially after I told her and Ana about my conversation with Kim.

"We don't know that at *all*," I said. "The chances of me getting into Canterwood are close to zero. I don't want you guys to be all sad about the new school year—it's going to be exciting and fun. Even if the world turns upside down and I get in somehow, we have all summer together. No matter what, we're besties forever." I looked at both of them. "Right?"

Brielle's frown disappeared. "Right." She smiled.

"Besties forever," Ana said, giggling and holding out her pinkie.

She, Brielle, and I tangled our pinkies together in a silent promise of bestie foreverness, smiling giant smiles. We went back to grooming our horses and tacked them up, resuming our chatter about school. But I couldn't shake the look I'd seen on Brielle's face. Why had she been so sure it was even possible I'd be gone?

We led our horses single file down the narrow aisle to the outdoor arena. Ana mounted first, easily lifting herself into Breeze's saddle. The always-calm strawberry roan mare stood still as Ana adjusted her stirrups. I loved

Breeze's wide blaze and socks. I'd ridden the mare before when Kim made us swap horses during a lesson. She'd been a smooth ride.

Brielle and I mounted next and the three of us let our horses walk through the entrance into the arena.

Dianna and Leah were already warming up inside. Our weekday lessons for my group consisted of just the five of us girls. There weren't any boys who rode in my class. We were all considered junior advanced riders at Briar Creek.

Ana, Brielle, and I spaced out our horses. I let Cricket on a loose rein to walk. The May air had a slight breeze and it felt good on my face, warm from grooming and tacking Cricket up.

The five of us warmed up, giving each other plenty of space to work, while we waited for Kim. It felt good to be back in the saddle and I was ready for whatever Kim threw at us.

I'd just eased Cricket from a slow canter to a trot when Kim walked into the arena. She stopped in the center, motioning for us to come closer to her. She wore a typical Kim outfit: a black-and-gray plaid button-down shirt, jeans, and a pair of well-worn paddock boots.

Leah, Dianna, Brielle, Ana, and I walked our horses

before Kim, stopping them far enough away to give her space to instruct.

"Good to see you all," Kim said. "Let's get to work right away—before the weather changes."

I looked up at the sky. It had already begun to fill with puffy, gray clouds. I doubted we'd even make it through the lesson without getting caught in the beginnings of a May downpour.

"We're going to leave the arena and practice on the jumping course set up on the grass," Kim said. "I'm going to time your rides. I'm looking for safe, clean, and fast rounds. Any questions?"

We shook our heads. I followed Brielle out of the arena with Ana and our other teammates trailing behind us. The tightness in my chest that had been almost paralyzing only months ago seemed to ease with every new jump I took. I was ready this time—no backing out.

Brielle and Ana were the only people outside Kim, Taylor, and my family I'd spoken to about my accident. Not that they hadn't already known. It had been in every sports section of every major newspaper and had run on a loop of slow-mo replays on HorseTV. The headlines that flashed on the TV's crawler danced around in my head: *Dressage champion Lauren Towers suffers from a serious accident during Red Oak Trials. . . .*

I took a deep breath, and let my exhaling air blow away the memory. The crawler scattered and broke apart, dissipating into nothing, the way Becca had taught me to do.

This was *not* something I needed to think about before a lesson—especially a jumping lesson. I let Cricket move into a brisk walk as she followed Zane to the outdoor course. The jumps we'd tackle were part of an advanced course. There were lots of turns, a couple of switchbacks, and Cricket's one fear about jumping—a ditch.

But I was ready to go and Cricket was, too. Her small body shivered with excitement as we made our way across the grassy field and reached the start of the course.

"All right," Kim said. "Brielle, you're up first. Then Dianna, Lauren, Ana, and Leah. You've all ridden this course before, so the jumps and their order should be familiar to you." Kim turned to Brielle and Zane. "Ready?"

"Ready," Brielle said with a confidence I wished I could reach over and take for myself.

Brielle was the best jumper in our group—with Dianna a close second. Brielle would jump over *anything* and everything in her path. Kim had spoken to her a couple of times about being more cautious, but it was embedded in Brielle's personality. She was an adrenaline junkie.

Still, despite the fact that Bri was crazy about jumping, she would *never* put her horse at risk. I'd seen enough of that around the show circuit—riders who didn't care about their horses and treated them like instruments or vehicles. Like the Mercedes or Jaguars they expected from their parents when they turned sixteen and still had their learner's permits.

My friends and I were all lucky enough to live in nice houses and were able to buy things that a lot of other kids couldn't afford. Most of the students at Yates Prep were just as lucky—otherwise, none of us would be able to afford Yates's tuition.

But one trait that the three of us shared was that all of our parents had taught us manners—and money hadn't come easily to any of them. I saw how hard my parents worked to have what they did and to provide for me. And my allowance didn't just come to me free. I worked for it by doing chores—laundry, dishes, even washing the car or taking out the trash. Bri's and Ana's parents were the same—it was something that brought us all together. Most of the kids at Yates were so spoiled they wouldn't even know what laundry detergent was.

It made all three of us crazy.

Brielle let Zane into a trot before easing him into a

collected canter. Her black breeches looked sharp against his white coat and her legs were positioned just right.

I sat tall in Cricket's saddle, watching Brielle prepare to jump. I hoped I could pick up a few tips from her round.

Zane, listening to Brielle, moved out of the large circle he'd been cantering in as she guided him toward the first jump. I knew the course well—I'd walked it many times and had made a diagram to study until I'd become comfortable with every aspect of it. Brielle and Ana had ridden with me—minus Dianna and Leah—so I could practice in front of trusted friends until I felt secure with my skills.

Brielle let Zane into a faster canter and they leaped the first vertical with ease. Zane was as great a jumper as Brielle—clean and careful. He drew his forelegs close to his chest with every jump and tucked his hind legs so his hooves wouldn't nick the rails.

The pair jumped two more verticals—each increasingly closer together—then turned back toward the beginning of the course to take an oxer. Brielle's timing was perfect—she knew just when to lift her body slightly out of the saddle. Her hands slid a few inches up Zane's neck. She gave him the rein he needed to take the oxer.

The other girls seemed as enraptured with Brielle's ride as I. Her black hair, having been taken down from its ponytail, streamed out behind her beneath her helmet like a silken, ebony flag. There wasn't a trace of bounce in her seat as she and Zane landed after each jump.

Kim clicked the stop button on the digital stopwatch in her hand as Brielle finished the last jump.

Brielle, smiling, patted Zane's shoulder as she slowed him. She stopped him beside us, looking to Kim for feedback.

"Well done," Kim said. "Your timing is impeccable. Zane was in control the entire time and your focus is remarkable. One thing to watch: your shoulders. They tend to creep up toward your ears after you come out of the two-point position."

"I felt that happening." Brielle nodded. "I'll definitely remember that next time. Thank you."

Kim smiled at her, then looked to Dianna. "You're up."

Dianna and her Quarter Horse, Zeya, ran into trouble on the course. The mare balked at the first jump of the triple combination and Dianna had to set her up all over again for the complicated jump. The refusal was enough to rattle Dianna, who couldn't get Zeya over the combo. The mare slowed to a near standstill before knocking the first part of the triple and Dianna couldn't get her going fast enough for momentum. They took out all three parts of the combination but made it through the rest of the ride without any more problems.

Disappointment was scrawled all over Dianna's face even though she praised Zeya, and I felt a sympathy pang drop my stomach to my feet. Dianna pushed her helmet down, pretending to adjust it, but I knew she was using the visor to partly hide her eyes. I felt her embarrassment and wanted to reach out and squeeze her hand—tell her I knew how it felt.

"Dianna, don't beat yourself up," Kim said, clearly sensing Dianna's mood. "Zeya had a bad round—it happens. You finished the rest of the course strong. You should be proud that you pulled it together after the triple."

Dianna lifted her head, her eyes meeting Kim's now. "Thanks, Kim. I feel a lot better now."

I could tell in Dianna's soft voice that it was true.

It was my turn.

Kim motioned to me and I walked Cricket away from the group. I sat deep in the saddle, tightening the reins to preempt Cricket from rushing. The mare had a bad habit of being able to sense my fear and, in turn, she'd rush jumps.

The first vertical, solid navy blue rails, reached us fast.

I rose just out of the saddle and took my weight off of Cricket's back. Even though she was small, the mare was a high jumper. She pulled her legs close to her body and I knew there were inches between us and the rails. Cricket landed cleanly on the other side, her hooves making a small *thud* in the grass.

One down! I smiled. *That* felt good!

Cricket and I focused on the next jump, plastic boards that looked wooden. Kim had placed a red bucket on either side in an effort to teach the horses not to be scared by objects they didn't expect to see on the course. Cricket didn't even seem to notice. She sailed over the jump with her ears pointed forward, focused on whatever was next.

I let her canter speed up as we approached, and Cricket took advantage of the extra rein without getting overexcited. Her experience, after spending years as a school horse, made me feel confident and adrenaline took over.

I wanted the best time.

And I wanted it to be by far.

Cricket and I surged over the fence and, without giving it a second thought, I let her into a hand gallop along the wide turn.

Kim hadn't said anything about *not* galloping. Besides,

there was plenty of room to slow before we reached the ditch.

Strides before the jump, I brought Cricket down to a medium canter, preparing myself to get her over the ditch. Cricket, who'd taken the course before, knew the jump was coming. She slowed, beginning to weave to the left. She pulled at the right rein in an attempt to weave and run out on the ditch.

I pulled her back into a straight line with steady pressure, tightening my legs against her sides.

Cricket's ears flicked back and forth. Her body tensed beneath me.

My own nerves started to surface.

You can do this—you've done it a zillion times.

Three deep breaths and we were in front of the ditch. I squeezed my boots against Cricket, leaning forward. The pretty bay didn't balk. She rocked back on her haunches and then—jumped!

Airborne.

It felt like much longer than the few seconds I knew to be true time. Our landing was smooth. We cantered our way through the rest of the course, heading to the final jump.

The last jump, a vertical, had plastic pinwheels on the

sides. The wheels spun in the gentle breeze and the blue-and-red wheels caught the sunlight. Cricket, emboldened after conquering the ditch, didn't respond to the pinwheels.

She stayed on track and jumped the tall vertical, landing with barely any sound at all, and then cantered back toward the group.

"Good girl!" I rubbed her neck and she snorted with what I knew to be pride.

I rode her through a few circles to let her muscles stretch and cool before I halted her. I looked at Kim, who had the stopwatch in hand.

"Lauren," Kim's voice sounded stern.

What? Oh, no—

"That . . . was a lovely ride," Kim finished.

I let out a frenetic breath. The truth was, after I'd done it, I'd felt sure Kim would be upset that I'd galloped on course. I knew we were technically allowed to, but Kim only wanted us to gallop when absolutely necessary.

I realized I still hadn't replied to Kim's compliment just as she began to speak again.

"Did the wind from your speed round give you a hearing problem?" Kim teased.

The other girls laughed.

"I was going to say that you took a gamble and it paid off. Sometimes, you have to take chances. It could have cost you a jump if you hadn't been able to slow Cricket. But you got her back under control and came in with the fastest time so far. Nice work." Kim pointed to Ana. "Your turn."

Ana and Leah had clean rides, too, but their times were still seconds slower than mine. Kim didn't have to say who had been the fastest with the cleanest ride, and I was glad when she didn't formally announce me as the winner. My successful ride had been the highlight of my week.

It made me feel like I hadn't disappointed anyone today—Mom and Dad especially—who had moved from Brooklyn to Union for me. They'd realized I needed a fresh start and Mom had applied for a job at a law firm just outside of Union. When she'd gotten the job, they'd taken me for a walk, asking how I felt about a new start at Briar Creek and a break from competition.

When they told me about one of Kim's students getting into Canterwood Crest Academy, it was a fact that sealed the deal. I'd already known a ton about Canterwood, so once I'd heard that this stable had a connection with the elite school, I couldn't have been more excited. Becca, on board for anything, had practically packed her stuff in a day. We'd never been happier than we were in Union.

"Nice work today, ladies," Kim said. She put her stopwatch into her back pocket. "Please cool out your horses and make sure they're fed and watered and have clean stalls before you leave. I'll see you at the next lesson."

We dismounted and followed Kim back to the stable.

"Whoa," Ana said, leading Breeze next to me. The mare, working off a slight hay belly, was sweating around her saddle pad. "You really went for it—that was awesome!"

"Totally," Brielle said, reaching my other side. "I didn't think you were going to do it, but you did. That was great."

"Guys, stop," I said, waving my free hand. "It was one good round. Your rides were clean, too."

Ana and Brielle both raised their eyebrows at the same time.

"Fine, fine," Brielle said in a singsong voice. "Whatever you say. Just don't do that every time. *I'm* the jumping queen."

"Got it," I said, laughing.

Walking our horses close together, the three of us talked and laughed the entire way back to the stable. And just like that, glee didn't feel like enough anymore.

6

WHAT IF . . . ?

I HEADED OUTSIDE TO THE STABLE PARKING lot and waited for Dad. Brielle and Ana left with Ana's mom. The two of them lived in the same neighborhood on the opposite side of town from me and my family.

While I waited for Dad, I played on my phone. I updated my Chatter status, an addiction of mine that Mom called the biggest waste of time ever, but I loved it. It was like a public diary.

A few months ago, I'd gone back and read a bunch of Chatter updates I'd posted over a year ago and realized something: they'd *all* been about riding. I thought back to some of the status updates as I leaned against the stable.

Swept the 3 day event! #1! 6:08 p.m.

Bad lesson. Fell off twice. Practicing 3x as long 2mrw. 11:14 p.m.

Starting @ new stable. Hope I like it. 2:09 a.m.

That had been my last round of riding-only related Chats. After I'd started at Briar Creek and enrolled at Yates, my Chats had changed. I scrolled through my last three Chats.

@AnaArtiste U have the English hmwk? 3:40 p.m.

Ahhh! @BrielleisaBeauty & @AnaArtiste I wish you guys were here right now! Just dropped ice cream on new black ballerina skirt—fashion fail! 12:15 p.m.

Waiting 4 news on something. Something kinda big. Rlly big, I guess. 9:07 p.m.

Now I had real-life friends following me, reading my thoughts, and my life didn't revolve solely around the stable.

My priorities had shifted, but it didn't mean I loved horses any less. Instead I found out I actually loved a bunch of things all at once.

And I was still as in love with riding as ever.

My phone buzzed and the symbol for a BBM appeared.

Taylor:

How was ur lesson?

I knew he would BBM me. Tay, an athlete like me, understood how important lessons and practice sessions were. We always BBM'd or spoke to each other after one of us had swim practice (him) or a riding lesson (me). He understood me in a way that no other guy did.

I typed back.

Lauren:

U know what? Awesome! My horse jumped rlly well—I'm happy. ☺

Taylor:

Your horse wasn't the only one who did well, LT. V cool!

Lauren:

Oh, pls. ;) Still @ BC I'm waiting 4 my dad. U?

Taylor:

Hmwk. Then backyard kickball w Sam. Mom asked me 2 so she could study.

Taylor's mom was going back to school to get her master's degree in psychology. She'd been at home with Taylor and his little brother, Sam, since they'd been born, but Mrs. Frost had decided to go back to school last fall.

Lauren:

Don't beat him 2 bad. ;)

Taylor

Ha. Plan = kick the ball into the Pearsons' yard and hope it lands in their garden—aka "the jungle." It'll take him hrs 2 find it.

Lauren:

Tay!

I laughed. Taylor talked a big game, but I knew he'd never play dirty with Sam. He loved his little brother—they'd probably have so much fun that they'd play until dark.

The sound of gravel crunching beneath tires made me look up from the BlackBerry's lit-up screen. Dad's black SUV crawled up the driveway. He always made sure to drive extra slow, so as not to spook the grazing horses.

Lauren:

Dad alert. TTYL & say hi 2 Sam.

Taylor:

Done. TTYL, LT.

I locked my phone's keypad before shoving it into my bag and climbing into the passenger seat.

"Hello, Laur-Bell," Dad said. He lifted my heavy bag from my struggling grasp, tossing it onto the backseat like it was filled with feathers. "How was your lesson?"

"Well . . ." I said. "We jumped today."

Dad's eyes shot over to me, then back to the driveway. "How'd that go?" Dad asked. I recognized the Dad-tone in his voice—the one that tried so hard to be casual.

"Really, *really* well." I exhaled.

Dad unclenched his fingers from their white-hard grip on the steering wheel.

"I had a clean round and the fastest time of anyone," I continued.

Dad rolled to a stop before pulling onto the main road. "That's great, Bell! I'm so proud. Wait 'til Mom hears this! What did Kim say to you?"

I played with the star-shaped stud in my ear. "She said I took a risk, but"—I rushed to get the rest out—"a good risk. Just by galloping before a jump. I haven't felt that good about jumping since, well, then."

I could practically see the brief wave of pain roll over Dad. But I also saw what followed: He shook it off and smiled a genuine smile at me.

"My girl looks happier than I've seen in a while—that's what I care about."

"Thanks, Dad." I grinned, looking down. A stack of mail was tucked in the partition between the seats next to Dad's travel mug.

I tried, unsuccessfully, to keep from staring.

"Anything good?" Now I heard my own forced casual voice.

I didn't have to say anything else.

"Oh, honey, I'm sorry," Dad said. "Those are just bills I brought to look over in case I had to wait for you."

Again, a bunch of different emotions washed over me.

Relief that there wasn't a yes, happiness that there wasn't a no. Impatience. And, stronger than the rest, grateful that today would still just be the day that I killed the jumps at practice.

"It's okay," I said. "I know it's going to be a few more weeks before I hear from Canterwood."

Dad glanced at me. "How are you feeling about Canterwood these days? We haven't talked about it in a while."

"Honestly? I don't know yet how I feel," I said. "It changes every time I think about it." I looked at the stack of envelopes. "Or every time I see mail," I added.

Dad laughed. "How do you mean?"

I let his question rattle around in my head before answering. "Well, half of the time, I'm disappointed when there's no acceptance letter. The other half of the time, I'm relieved there's no letter because it could mean a no. And then I go back and forth about getting in. The school is so amazing, Dad. I want it—I want to be chosen so bad. But then . . . what happens if I actually get what I want?"

"Then you'll go and you'll do great," Dad said, his eyes crinkling as he smiled.

Suddenly my seat belt was constricting my chest. I tried to pull on it, but it only tangled and locked in place.

"Maybe I won't, though! I could get in and completely drop the ball. Academics there are hard. Everyone talks about how tough classes are and the pace there is so fast. I might not be able to keep up with school *and* riding. What if I fail, Dad?" I paused, feeling my fair cheeks burn with the weight of all my unanswered questions. "What if I fall?"

"Laur-Bell," Dad leaned over and touched my hand. "You're a smart girl. Yates is *not* an easy school, and you're taking the most difficult and fullest course load possible there. I know how hard you work."

"What about falling?" I asked again.

Dad laughed. "Where's the girl I just picked up from practice? The one who got in the car and told me how she kicked everyone's butt at jumping today?"

Smiling, I leaned back into my seat and stared out the window at the cars and trucks whizzing by on the highway.

"She's right here," I asserted.

Now I wanted that envelope to come more than ever.

7
LAUREN'S ADDICTION

I ❤ *wknds! So xcited 2 hang w Tay 2nite! 5:18 p.m.*

Once I updated my Chatter status, I put my phone on my desk. Taylor and I were going to the movies and then out to grab a slice of pizza. His dad would be here to pick me up at seven. I needed something distracting—seven seemed *so* far away!

I picked up my baby blue leather messenger bag, letting out an *ooof!* as I set it on the bed. It was so full, it barely closed, and I was sure the straps were going to break. I pulled out the books I needed for the weekend's homework. Each book was bigger than the one before.

Math.

Science with workbook.

French II textbook.

English textbook and *Animal Farm*.

Art history.

American history.

And those were just the books I needed to read from. The rest of the weekend's homework was posted on Yates's Web site. To top it off, at some point I needed to log in and post a discussion question for creative writing *and* offer replies to at least four other students' questions.

In general, weekends definitely weren't work-free in the Towers's household. Becca had started her homework early this morning, so she was already out with her bestie, Casey. I'd decided to ease into the day. I slept in, watched a little TV, then spent some time on IM chatting with Ana and Brielle.

I stacked my books in a neat pile on my desk and decided to dive into the art history that would be due on Tuesday. But for me, homework was a finely tuned ritual and I could not even write one word until I had my go-to homework drink. Brielle's was Diet Coke. Ana loved cappuccinos with sugar. Lots and *lots* of sugar. I'd actually *gagged* when I'd accidentally taken a tiny sip from her cup once. That was a mistake I'd never make again for fear of going into a sugar coma.

I headed downstairs to the kitchen. I could tell by the

shiny marble tiles that Ellen had been here this morning. I looked around the house. Everything was sparkly clean, exactly the way I liked it. I reached into the light wooden cabinet above the stove and took out last year's Christmas present from Aunt Cathy—a stainless steel Krups teapot with a black rubber handle. I filled the pot with water from our Brita filter and turned the gas stove on high until the tips of the mostly blue flames licked the outer circumference of the teapot.

Next, I opened another cabinet door and took out a wicker basket that had been painted bronze. I carried the basket to the breakfast nook and sat at the small round table, peering into my basket. I treated the basket as if it contained diamonds, but what was really inside was tea. Tea, tea, and more tea. I had boxes and bags of every imaginable kind—herbal, black, green, red, white.

I'd started drinking tea back when we lived in Brooklyn—mostly because our house was a three-floor brownstone with just one tiny radiator to heat the entire place. It had always been so freezing that the entire family started drinking tea, just to have a warm cup clasped between their palms at all times.

Tea, Dad always told me, kept you warm from the inside out. Back then, Becca and I were too young and, therefore, banned from caffeinated tea. So Mom always had a box of our favorite flavors of caffeine-free Celestial Seasonings on the center of the kitchen table. Becca's was Gingerbread Spice. And mine was Sugar Cookie Sleigh Ride—it tasted best with actual sugar in it.

Now, even though our house was warm, tea had become a total obsession. All of my friends and family knew to get me tea whenever they saw a unique flavor. It was like a game for them to find a kind I hadn't tried. I even kept a tea journal and recorded each kind I tasted, and I rated them from $+ \bigstar \bigstar \bigstar \bigstar \bigstar$ to $- \bigstar$. Sometimes tea was so bad it needed a negative star. In my bedroom on my bookcase, I had books about tea, and I'd learned interesting facts about it—like the history of the leaves, how to make a perfect cup, and where to find the most exotic teas.

I had tea for all occasions: pulling all-nighters (Vanilla Black Twinings), calming down before bed (chamomile Bigelow), rainy days (Perfectly Pear White Celestial Seasonings), cold weather (Winter Spice Twinings), bad days (Sugar Cookie Sleigh Ride Celestial Seasonings—it was still my favorite), and sick days (Peppermint Celestial Seasonings).

It was Saturday night, so I wanted something spiked with caffeine and cooling since it was warm out.

I moved boxes of Tazo, Celestial Seasonings, Twinings, and Harney & Sons until I found what I wanted—Organic Green Tea With Mint.

Très parfait. Caffeinated and cooling. Ooh la la!

I took the pyramid-shaped tea bag out of the larger zipped bag and got up when the teapot started to whistle. Ana and Brielle loved to tease me about my tea habit. They thought it was weird that I had to use a stove-top teakettle for tea and called me a snob—pushing the tips of their noses in the air and lifting their chins when I wouldn't use a microwave to heat water just because it was faster. I had tried to explain that there was something about the ritual of boiling the water on the stove that I liked, but they only rolled their eyes.

I picked out my favorite homework teacup—a powder blue one with a small, delicate daisy painted on it. It had a matching saucer and tiny stirring spoon. I took my cup of steaming tea upstairs and placed it on my bedside table, beside the magazines I was reading before I went to bed. I had a mix of everything—fashion, gossip, and horses.

I opened the double doors to my closet and flipped up the light switch. My closet was the most embarrassing example of my inner neat freak. My clothes were arranged by color, even down to shades within the same color category. I'd always *loved* clothes, but most of my shopping had been limited to online purchases that Dad and I quickly added to various carts while I traveled on an insanely busy show circuit. Back then, I'd had practically zero time to go to actual stores. But in Brooklyn, Mom and I could never resist the local boutiques or making special trips to the bigger stores in Manhattan like Bloomingdale's, Bergdorf, or—on a very special occasion—Barneys.

Now that I'd taken a break from showing, I'd spent a lot of time doing things I'd never had time for when I was younger—even simple things like exploring my neighborhood, shopping with my friends in actual stores, where I could actually try on clothes, and going to free concerts in the park.

I took in each section. The black and white sections, which were adjacent to each other, I thought of as my "Audrey Hepburn sections" because she wore a lot of those two simple colors and made them look stunning. The section I thought of as the "sister section" was all shades of purple (Becca's favorite color) and blue (my favorite color). I selected an outfit for tonight while my tea cooled. I took my time, running my fingers over all of the different fabrics and cuts, each item hanging from a silk ivory hanger adorned by a tiny ribbon-bow where the base of the hook was.

I started at the Audrey Hepburn section and plucked a black, summery A-line skirt covered with dozens of *fleur-de-lis* designs that were stitched on with fine, silver thread. I stayed in the same section to select a delicate scoop-neck tissue tee in soft white.

I grabbed a cardigan sweater from the sister section—a grape-y purple button-down with sparkly rhinestone buttons that Becca convinced me to purchase from J.Crew just last weekend. I felt the thin microfiber material between my thumb and index fingers, grateful to be holding a sweater my sister had picked out, that I'd tried on and realized ran small and swapped it for a size up, one that we bought in the store together and that I assumed she wanted me to get because it was her favorite color and she'd borrow it before I even got to wear it once.

A sweater that surprised me because, here I was, cutting off the tags to wear it out on a date with Tay, my boyfriend—not some guy I met and competed against in the arena. Just a boy I liked hanging out with—an athlete, like me, who got why I had to take a break after my fall, who got why I only drank tea with kettle water, and why spending a whole night just watching a movie and going out for a slice of pizza felt like a luxury. A boy Lauren Towers a year and a half ago wouldn't even have time to text.

An ambulance siren wailed, making me feel queasy. I'd been dreading today for a while—it was the grand opening of a new hospital a few blocks away. It had been all over the news that today had been Union County Hospital's ribbon-cutting ceremony. I hated the h-word, and just hearing the far-off siren brought back memories I didn't want to think about.

I sat down on the closet floor, squeezing my eyes shut as I leaned my back against the shoe wall. Memories of a time before sweater shopping and movie dates and getting to know more about a boy than how many blue ribbons he'd snagged wanted to invade! Memories about a girl before she fell, before it was splashed across the news in slow-motion on every channel. A busy, thrilling, whirlwind competitive time and the way it all halted so fast. The sound of a shocked, worried crowd, those memories—the darkest, scariest ones—I'd tried to stop thinking about were coming back.

The ambulance siren I'd just heard sounded just like the ones I'd heard when I'd been on the ground. Everyone around me had looked so worried.

"I'm fine," I assured them.

Mr. Wells asked me to wiggle my fingers and toes, which I did without a problem.

"Everything feels fine," I said again. But something wasn't right. I felt . . . fear.

But this had been my first serious spill. There hadn't been any warning at all. One second, I was galloping toward a jump—the final jump. My body had already gotten comfortable, and in my head I was excited about finishing.

The next thing I knew, I was lying on the ground, aching all over.

All of a sudden, the world was moving again. All I wanted was stillness.

Two paramedics—or maybe three?—placed a brace around my neck and loaded me carefully onto a stretcher.

What people would remember most was the way I protested. This was unnecessary, I insisted. The last thing I wanted was to go to the hospital where strangers could keep staring. I really just wanted to curl up under every blanket on my bed and sleep away what had happened.

Maybe if I slept, I remembered reasoning, the fear would disappear.

But I didn't go home. Instead, I spent a night in the hospital. "For observation." The doctors were worried about possible head trauma. I was released the next day with clearance to ride again as soon as my body felt ready.

I barely spoke the next week. Whenever Mom and Dad brought up riding, I made up excuse after excuse.

Too much homework.

I was still sore.

Skyblue probably needed more of a break.

But it wasn't Skyblue—it was me.

The accident had shaken me to my bones. My invincibility was gone. But every night in the Brooklyn apartment, the accident replayed over and over in my head—Skyblue balking and my flying like a rag doll over his head, crashing hard to the ground.

I wasn't scared to ride, but jumping was a different story. It didn't sound like something I wanted to do for a *long* time. Cross-country and stadium jumping, though, were part of three-day eventing. And if I wanted to be part of the team, I knew I'd have to do all three. Dressage alone wasn't an option.

I knew I'd have to make a decision.

8

MY BOYFRIEND
THE LIAR

I YANKED MYSELF OUT OF MY MEMORY-slash-daydream and looked at the clock. Forty-five minutes before Taylor's dad was supposed to arrive to pick me up.

I hopped off my bed and dashed into the bathroom. I hovered close enough to the mirror to fog it with my breath. I examined my pale skin for any imperfections that may have popped up since I'd last checked the mirror.

Lucky for my date, nothing but pale skin and a faint spray of half a dozen freckles on each cheek.

I pulled out my black crushed-velvet vanity chair with a cushy seat and sat in front of my makeup counter. I turned on the makeup lights, unfurling my three-way mirror. It had three different settings—daytime, school (fluorescent lights), and night.

I set it on night and grabbed my CoverGirl foundation—the lightest shade they made, called "porcelain." My makeup was a soft, feminine mix of designer and drugstore brands. Becca teased me for it, but I did my makeup the same exact way every time. First, I laid it all out in order of application. I smoothed an ultra-thin layer of foundation on my forehead, cheeks, and chin, followed by concealer dabbed under my eyes.

Next, I picked up my wide snow-white Clinique brush and ran it over my shimmery peach Nars blush and dusted a hint of color over my cheekbones, nose, and chin. I lined my eyes—a superfine line—with MAC's Smolder.

In the glass jar hand-painted with pretty swirls, I picked out my expert MAC eye shadow brush. I dabbed it in light-colored shimmer eye shadow and used the brush to dust it across my lids. A darker shade of brown closer to my lash line defined my eyes. For eyelashes, I used a trick I'd read in a fashion magazine: I blasted my eyelash curler with warm air from my hairdryer for a few seconds. Then, I clamped the curler on my lashes. The heat from the hairdryer would help hold the curl longer. After a coat of waterproof Maybelline brown-black mascara, my eyes were done.

Finally, I dusted loose powder across my T-zone and

applied a coat of Sephora's Forever Pink gloss. I inspected the tube—three-fourths of the way gone—and made a note on my light blue Kate Spade mini-notepad to pick up a new one ASAP. It was one of my staples: a barely there pink with lots of light-catching flecks of shimmer. In other words, *la glose parfait* (aka perfect gloss) for my Friday night movie date with Tay.

Next stop: hair. I stood in front of the antique floor-length mirror in the corner of my room. The girl inside the chipped ivory frame needed straight hair tonight. I wanted zero waves, not even beauty curl. I plugged in my ceramic flatiron, which took only seconds to heat. I sprayed my hair with a dewy mist of Bumble and bumble Prep to protect it from heat damage, then clipped it up into sections. Twenty minutes later, my hair was down and straight, without being too straight.

It looked shiny and smooth. By now, I'd perfected the art of a good flat iron. The secret was to lift straight up rather than pull down. I'd finally learned the right way in Union. It gave my hair natural body without being poofy. Pulling straight down made hair look limp and lifeless. It was one of the EBTs (essential beauty tricks) that Ana, Brielle, and I swapped on a regular basis. I rubbed my fingers through my smoother, straight hair, spreading a lightly perfumed shine serum throughout.

In record time, I dressed and now it was time to accessorize. I grabbed a long silver delicate chain that held an oversized locket. I grabbed another necklace to layer with it. The locket was an antique-looking heart and the other was chunkier and made up of dozens of shiny, black hematite stones, with smaller, matte balls in between each stone. I knotted the hematite necklace with the locket so the layers were at the right spot and they fell perfectly into place.

I redid one last check of hair-slash-makeup, grabbed my distressed silver purse, then calmly headed to the front door. I was right on time and ready to bask in the fluttery feeling I got before every date with Taylor. A movie and dinner sounded perfect and was exactly the type of thing I was in the mood for.

Tonight any thoughts about getting into Canterwood (or not), studying for classes, competitive riding, and dressage technique would all have to be put on pause.

My phone blinked and it was a mention of my name on Chatter by "TFrost," Tay.

Happy 2 be going out w @LaurBell! 6:55 p.m.

I typed a quick reply. *@TFrost See you soon!* ♥ 6:56 p.m.

BURKHART

"Mom!" I called. "Taylor's dad will be here in two seconds."

Mom appeared around the corner. She eyed my outfit, doing her Mom-slash-lawyer daughter-scan for anything inappropriate. Her smile told me that whatever test she'd just given me, I'd passed. I blew her a kiss and headed for the door.

"Remember to check in with us throughout the night, especially if your plans change," Mom said. "Be home by curfew."

"I will. We're just going to see a movie and grabbing food after. I'll text you after the movie."

Even though I'd never been grounded in my life, my mom was still a lawyer and it made her feel better to have set family rules like my nine-thirty curfew. I'd never broken her rules the way Charlotte had, but I didn't mind them if it made her feel better about things like movie dates and slumber parties with the besties.

Mom nodded. "Sounds good. Lauren?"

I turned to face her.

"Have fun," she said.

I smiled, waved good-bye, and walked onto the front porch. I was just about to sit on the porch swing when Taylor's parents' Suburban pulled into our driveway.

I slid my keyboard-locked BlackBerry into my purse and walked down the sidewalk to their SUV. I tried my best not to rush—I didn't want to seem overeager and held my back straight.

I hoped that the car's headlights caught some of the shimmer I'd carefully applied. I wanted to impress Taylor tonight, of course, but even more than that, I wanted to feel *pretty*.

I didn't usually obsess over my looks, but felt okay to be a stylish girl that anyone would be proud to go out with tonight. And, for some reason, I *felt* pretty. Not like a competitive equestrian on the verge of finding out life-changing news, or an organized honors student who kept a neat closet and turned her homework in early. Just a pretty, carefree girl, out with her boyfriend on a Friday night.

"Hi, Mr. Frost," I said, climbing into the backseat of the SUV. Taylor was already seated in the back. His smile widened and he placed a hand briefly over mine.

"You look *great*," he said low, so only I could hear. I beamed at him, suddenly feeling even prettier and mounted a bashful smile.

"Hello, Lauren," Mr. Frost said. The guy didn't know how to *not* be formal. Even on a Friday night he wore a suit and tie. It was like he was on his way to a fancy dinner rather than dropping us off at the movies. "You look very nice tonight, as always," Mr. Frost told me.

"Thank you for picking me up," I said. "And thank you." I smiled at Taylor when I spoke. I didn't want to act too girlfriendy in the car. Especially not in front of Mr. Frost. Plus, even though he'd paid me the exact compliment I'd hoped for, it was in an adult "aren't you cute" way and Taylor's face had reddened at his dad's compliment.

"You're welcome," Mr. Frost said. He left my driveway and pulled onto the street, navigating the twists and turns out of my neighborhood.

"Hey," I said softly, finally feeling like I could talk to Taylor without his dad thinking I was rude.

"Hey," Taylor said, turning in the seat next to me and taking my hand. He held it down so his dad couldn't see. I noticed that he'd put extra effort into making his messy-on-purpose hair look nice. And he wore perfectly broken-in jeans and a nice black button-down I'd never seen before.

"You look really nice, Tay," I said, adding something else quickly so he couldn't respond. "And I'm excited about the movie. I'm in the mood for something fun—an action flick."

"I thought you BBM'd me the wrong title by mistake or something," Taylor said, arching his eyebrows. "Usually, when you pick a movie, it's kind of . . ."

I turned to him, eyebrows raised to match his. "Kind of *what*?" I challenged.

"You know, kind of a chick flick."

"Oh, puh-lease!" I dropped my jaw in feigned shock. "The last movie we saw was—"

"A chick flick," Taylor finished, grinning.

"I don't remember that at all," I teased. "But even if you are right, which you're not—" I hesitated. "Well, okay, okay. The last one was. But the one before that wasn't."

Taylor rubbed his thumb across the top of my hand. He winked at me.

"You like?" I asked, giggling. His mock exasperated look made me laugh harder and harder. I hadn't laughed like this in forever.

"There's this epic Spielberg movie coming out next fall," Taylor said, leaning closer to me. "It's already getting so much buzz and I want to see if we can convince our parents to let us get in line for a midnight showing."

"I'm in," I said. "That sounds fun!"

Taylor's blue eyes held my gaze. "And that's why you're my girlfriend. Always game for anything."

A look passed across his face. If I didn't know him better, I would have said he'd looked sad. But then it was gone. He smiled at me, the strange, unfamiliar expression gone. He pulled out his iPod, eager for me to listen to a new song he'd downloaded.

I tried to concentrate on the song and convince myself I'd imagined the look. Nothing had just happened and, even if it had, it's not like we could talk about it now in front of Tay's dad.

I kept the conversation light for the rest of the ride.

If something was bothering Taylor, he'd tell me once we had more privacy—once we were out of the car and alone together. *But,* I told myself again, *there is probably nothing to even talk about.*

It was my imagination, I was sure of it. Maybe I was just too Type A to let everything be fun and completely stress free. Even when I set out to have a fun night, my brain invented things to worry about.

Everything was perfect. Taylor and I were out on a carefree Friday-night movie date and nothing was going to stop us from enjoying the night.

Right?

8

CRYSTAL BALL, ANYONE?

ONCE WE GOT OUT OF THE SUV, TAYLOR started for the theater. I walked beside him, checking to make sure his dad had left.

Before we reached the theater entrance, I put my hand in his, pulling him to a stop and out of the way of people traffic.

"What's up?" he asked. His features looked soft in the setting sun.

"Did something happen, in the car? I'm probably wrong, but I thought I saw a strange look. Is everything okay?"

"I'm out with my girlfriend on Friday night," Taylor said. "Everything's *better* than *okay*."

But now there was something in his voice—an odd

tone that made me wonder if he was being 100 percent honest with me. "Are you sure?" You can talk to me about anything—no matter what. Right?"

"Right," he said.

I waved my hand in a dismissive gesture. "No, I figured I was seeing thing. But . . ."

"But?" he prompted.

"It's just, you know . . ."

Taylor paused, taking a breath. "I know. I mean, maybe something popped into my brain in the car that bothered me just for a second. I didn't want you to see it. But it's not a big deal and tonight was about just having *fun*. Let's forget it for now. Okay?"

He held out his hand for me to take and angled his body back toward the theater.

I gave him my best understanding smile, but my feet felt cemented to the ground. I tried to keep my tone light as I spoke.

"Well, now you have to tell me. I want to know."

Taylor ran a hand through his thick blond hair. "It's really dumb."

"If something's bugging you, it's not dumb. Tay, you can tell me."

I looked at him, waiting.

Finally, he sighed.

"I don't want to keep anything from you," Taylor said. "But I feel like a jerk. I want you to be accepted to Canterwood—you deserve it and it would be an amazing opportunity. But at the same time, I don't want you to leave. That would mean—"

I touched his arm. "I know," I said. "It's hard not to think about what might happen. Funny how we were both thinking about it, but not talking about it. I kept trying to bring it up, but I couldn't figure out how. Not that I even think I have a chance of getting accepted."

His Converse rolled loose gravel over the pavement, making a cereal-crunching noise.

"So, do we talk about what happens if you do get in?" he asked. "Or do we wait?"

I caught my bottom lip between my teeth. I let out a nervous breath before answering. "Getting in is *such* a long shot," I said. "I think we should wait, if that's okay. If I'm actually chosen to fill the *one* open seat available, then we talk about what happens. *If* I ever get in," I added. "Which I won't."

"It's a plan," Taylor agreed. "But, Laur." His eyes locked on mine. "For what it's worth, I don't doubt for a second that you'll get in."

He took my hand and led me toward the theater. I held his hand tight, smiling but feeling shaken. I'd known we'd have to eventually have this conversation, but I hadn't expected it tonight. And I'd been doing such a good job convincing myself I'd never get in, it didn't even seem like a conversation worth having. But hearing Taylor say it out loud, it suddenly seemed plausible. I might get accepted. He'd sounded so sure when I'd been equally convinced I'd just get rejected. Now I wondered what would happen to me and Tay if he was right and I got accepted. I squeezed my eyes shut for a second, trying to push away the unanswered question.

Taylor and I got in line for tickets. The small theater, with only two screens, was bustling. At the counter, Taylor bought our tickets and handed me one. I loved the quaint theater. Tay didn't like how small it was, but I preferred it. The cream-colored walls had framed photos of the theater in various stages of renovation over the years.

My favorite was the black-and-white photo, yellowing a little around the edges, that showed the theater when it had first opened. A man, a young boy, and a woman stood together, all smiling at the camera. Everyone knew they were the family who had opened the theater and kept it as a family-run business all these years, refusing buy outs from the large chain theaters.

"You got tickets, I'll get snacks," I said. I knew all of Taylor's favorites.

"Deal," he said.

We walked over to the concession stand and I ordered a bucket of extra-buttery popcorn, a giant Sprite, peanut M&M's, and Necco Wafers.

We walked down the gray carpet, and the usher took our ticket stubs and pointed us toward the theater. The lights were already dimmed, and people filed inside. The previews hadn't started yet.

We walked down the aisle that had rope lighting on the sides. Taylor and I sat in the middle—our favorite spot. I sat down and put the Sprite in the cup holder between us. Without a word, I unwrapped my Neccos while Taylor opened his M&M's. So far, the night had not gone anything like I'd hoped. First, I'd been unprepared to talk about the possibility of going away when Tay had brought it up. And now, despite the fact that we'd agreed not to even think about it yet, things felt off between us. We'd barely looked at each other since he'd handed me my movie ticket.

I caught myself chewing on the corner of my bottom

lip—a nervous habit I'd developed at my old stable—and closed my mouth, teeth clenched together. I put a smile on my face, determined to have the fun Friday-night date I'd been looking forward to all day. Maybe it wasn't too late to turn this night around.

I braved a glance toward Tay, turning up the wattage of my smile. "Hey," I said, taking his hand. "I'm glad we're here."

I saw a brief flash of his adorable smile before it faded and turned back to the look I'd seen earlier in the evening. "Me too," he said with less enthusiasm than I hoped. He gave my hand a squeeze before taking it back to pick up the Sprite and take a sip.

Once darkness came over the theater and the previews began, I let my smile drop. Everything in my life really did depend on Canterwood.

My friends were waiting to see if I got accepted. My family, especially Becca, went through the daily ups and downs while I waited. Even my teammates at Briar Creek could lose me next fall.

As for Taylor, he would either have a long distance girlfriend or . . . Unexpected tears blurred my vision. Taylor would either have a long-distance girlfriend or we'd break up.

CHOSEN

It wasn't even something I could think about *now*. It was too soon. If I did end up getting accepted to Canterwood, I didn't want to look back at the time I'd spent with Taylor and know I'd wasted it being upset the whole time. I couldn't handle thinking about this.

In the darkness between previews and the start of the movie, I reached for Taylor and kissed him. This time, it was *Tay* who grabbed *my* hand. And this time, he didn't let go.

As the movie started, my anxiety slowly melted away. Canterwood, riding, unpleasant memories—everything seemed to be moving farther and farther away. Maybe things would change soon, and maybe they wouldn't. But for now, I felt comfortable and happy living the way someone my age should: in the moment.

Ninety minutes later, the lights came on and we walked out of the theater.

"What an awesome movie!" I said. "I was on the edge of my seat the whole time."

"Oh, man, totally agree," Taylor said. "It felt like it was five minutes long."

We tossed our empty candy wrappers and half-eaten popcorn into the trash can and headed outside to wait for Taylor's dad.

"I can't *wait* until I can drive," Taylor said. For as long as I'd known him, Taylor had been *obsessed* with cars. He had a closet full of models he'd put together when he was younger and the walls in his room were covered with posters of cars. (He'd told me a bunch of times, but I could never remember what they were!)

"Three years and you'll have your permit," I said. "That's not too far away."

Taylor's eyes brightened from the light of the street lamp. "What's not too far away is *dinner*. I'm so glad you chose Italian. I'm starving."

Taylor's dad drove up to us at the curb.

We got inside the SUV and, feeling happy and excited after our great movie date, I watched out the window at the quiet side streets we passed on the way to the restaurant. Union was a small town, populated by only a few thousand people. Tonight, it looked as though most of the people that were out were either high school kids or students from the nearby community college.

Once we reached La Bruschetta, the best (well, *only*) Italian restaurant in Union, Taylor's dad told us he'd be back in an hour and a half to pick us up.

Tay pulled open the restaurant door for me. La Bruschetta had the perfect date-night ambience. The rustic wooden tables all had flickering votive candles on top, which provided most of the dim room's lighting. The polished hardwood floors and cranberry-red cloth napkins matched the brick walls nicely. The entire restaurant smelled like garlic, marinara, and basil. The pizzas were all made in a large, open brick oven that was out in the open in the back of the room so you could watch them being made and going in to bake.

"Table for two," Tay told the waitress who greeted us at the door.

She smiled, looking at us like we were two puppies in a pet store window and grabbed two menus before walking us to our table.

Taylor pulled out my chair and motioned for me to sit. You wouldn't know by looking at him, but Tay was one of the most polite boys I'd ever met in Syracuse, Brooklyn, *or* Union. He looked like any cute jock—in good shape, dirty-blond hair with lighter white-blond at the ends, and his perpetually tan face from playing outdoor sports year round.

But his mother, who was *huge* into manners, brought him up well, and he was always pulling out chairs for me, opening doors for me, and offering to pick up the tab. I let him do everything but the last one—I believed that guys shouldn't do all the paying. Still, I secretly loved that he offered every time. Along with his *killer* sense of humor and soft spot for animals (especially cats—my favorite animal after horses!), his old-school politeness-slash-manners were among my favorite of his qualities.

We'd been seated at a cozy table in the back. The votive candles flickered—the flame seeming to match the rhythm of people talking and laughing around us.

A waiter brought us a bread basket, along with whipped packets of butter and a butter knife.

I reached for a roll and broke it open. Steam rose, curling into the air. The butter melted right away and I took a small, polite bite.

"Mmm," I said. "I love warm bread. I'd be happy just eating the entire basketful."

Taylor, ever the boy, was already working on his second roll. "Me too," he said unnecessarily. "But since we're here, I guess we should look at the menu." He grinned. "Got anything in mind?"

I scanned the pizza list. "Are you in the mood for pizza? We could each choose a topping for a side."

"I'm *always* in the mood for pizza," said Tay. "Does double cheese sound good on my side?"

"Only if pepperoni and black olives sound good on mine."

"Done." Taylor closed the menu just as the waiter came back.

"Good evening," he said. "I'm Don and I'll be your server tonight. May I start you off with some drinks?"

"Please," said Taylor. "And we're ready to order, too."

"Excellent. For you, miss?" I noticed the absence of any pen or notepad. I couldn't imagine doing such hard work and not even needing to write an order down. I shuddered to think what would happen if I ever became a waitress at La Bruschetta. No one here had ever written down an order. Without pen and notepad, I'd never stay organized enough to do my job. I'd get fired after one night!

"Miss?" Don repeated.

"I'll have a Dr Pepper, please," I said.

Don turned to Taylor. "I'd like a Coke and we'd like to share a medium pizza, half double cheese and half pepperoni and black olive."

"Wonderful. I'll be right back with your drinks," Don said, smiling.

Once he'd left, Tay looked at me inquisitively. "What's going on up there?" he asked kindly, tapping his own head.

"That's not the first time this week I've caught you day-dreaming. Something on your mind?"

I laughed, my face feeling a little warm. Memories, good *and* bad, had been rising to the surface while I waited for my Canterwood letter. But now that I was sure it would be a rejection, I felt sure they would start to quiet soon enough. After all, I'd been caught daydreaming again, but this time it had been about what an awful waitress I'd make. But I didn't want to waste a second of our date on something silly.

So instead, I said, "You caught me, and you're right. I've been living in my head a lot lately—mostly thinking about Canterwood. But," I added quickly, before I had to see a sad look even begin to cross Taylor's face, "now that I know what Kim told them, I am totally focused on the now. You caught me, though, it's true. But this time I wasn't thinking about anything Canterwood related. Not at all."

Taylor leaned toward me over the table. His elbows rested on the table and he laced his fingers together a couple of inches above his latest unfinished roll. I was relieved when a smile bloomed on his face. "No?" he said. "Then what were you thinking about, Laur-Bell?"

Without hesitation, I replied. "I was thinking about how great this night is turning out to be."

It wasn't a total lie. I *had* thought about that earlier.

"You're just saying that because of the extra cheese coming your way," he said.

His face was so serious, I erupted with laughter and, in turn, so did he.

"Maybe a little," I said.

From there, Taylor and I jumped into conversation about school, swimming, and riding.

"You're really going to dive from the highest board next meet?" I asked. "Your poor girlfriend must be insanely nervous!"

Taylor laughed. "Why? She doesn't have to do it."

"True. But she has to watch, which she promised to do, of course. I mean, she told me how proud she was of you. She might have to watch between the fingers covering her eyes."

That made Taylor smile.

"I'll be careful," he said. "But don't repeat that—I want the team at Madison to stay scared."

I nodded, pretending to be serious. "Consider it top secret. Madison will be shaking by the time they hit the pool."

"Speaking of top secret," Taylor said. "How'd your last lesson go?"

"Great," I said. "But I didn't tell you what I found out from Kim before."

I'd said I hadn't wanted to talk about Canterwood, but telling Tay this would ease his mind.

Taylor looked at me, curious.

"Kim told me that in my application, she told the committee about my jumping problem. So now there's *definitely* no way I'm getting in. Who would want me after my accident?"

"Laur." Taylor shook his head. "That's so not true. Canterwood would be lucky to have you, and the second they review your application, they'll realize it."

"We're going to have to agree to disagree, huh?" I said.

Tay nodded, swirling the ice in his glass with his straw. He held up his Coke and I did the same. We clinked our glasses together and smiled. If Tay believed in me, it made me feel a glimmer of hope that maybe, just maybe, I had a shot at Canterwood after all.

Taylor's dad picked us up from the restaurant right on time. When we got to my house, I opened my door. I got out and turned to Taylor.

"Talk to you later," I said. "Thanks for such an amazing night."

Tay, aware of the never-kiss-in-front-of-parents rule, grinned at me. "I had an awesome time. And my girlfriend picked the most perfect movie *ever*." His tone was teasing.

I pretended to look shocked.

"But then again," he said, his voice soft. "Any movie is perfect when I'm with you."

I brushed my thumb lightly against his chin, smiling. "'Night, Tay."

I headed for my front door. Elation tugged at me.

Even though I was 99 percent sure what I would see, I wished I had a crystal ball to look into my future.

9

WELCOME TO
MY WORLD

THE NEXT MORNING I WOKE UP RIGHT before my alarm clock started buzzing. I hopped out of bed and pulled on fawn-colored breeches and a purple T-shirt dotted with small black hearts. Mom was already in her office, so I waved at her as I walked to the kitchen. I put my phone on the table and poured myself a giant bowl of Cheerios before sitting down. I had a riding lesson in an hour, but surprisingly, I wasn't dreading it. Sunday group lessons had always been my favorite. I spooned cereal into my mouth and opened the group chat with Brielle and Ana on BlackBerry Messenger.

Lauren:

U guys awake?

My phone buzzed when I was halfway through my cereal bowl.

Brielle:

Woke up late!! But gonna b on time. Ana? Hellooo?

Ana:

Here! Couldn't brush my teeth & type @ the same time. I'll b on time 2. U, L?

Lauren:

Same. Prob early. Gotta go find Dad then leaving. C u guys there!

Brielle:

☺

Ana:

Double ☺

I finished my cereal, rinsed the bowl, and put it in the dishwasher. Then I headed to Dad's usual Sunday morning spot—the back porch. Once I walked through the sliding glass door, I saw Dad exactly where I expected. He sat on a lounge chair, book in hand and a mug of strong black coffee beside him. Tea was definitely more my style—tea with sugar. Or Splenda. Splenda was sweeter than sugar when I needed maximum sweetness.

"Ready to go already?" Dad asked, peering up at me from his novel. It was a thriller—Dad was totally into action novels.

"Yep. Oh! And I'll probably trail ride with Ana and

Brielle after we're done, so would it be okay if you picked me up a couple of hours after practice ends?"

Dad climbed out of his chair, nodding as he picked up his coffee. "Sure, sweetie. A trail ride sounds like a nice idea."

Once we were on the road, I texted Brielle and Ana again.

Lauren:

We're going 2 creek aftr lesson, rite? It's gonna b hot out.

Ana:

I want to! 😊 *Brielle?*

Brielle:

Def. I just got off IM w a certain someone, so I need major girl talk . . .

Ana and I messaged nearly at the same second.

Lauren:

WHAT???

Ana:

Will?! U talked 2 Will???

Brielle made us wait an excruciatingly long time before she replied.

Brielle:

Not telling u over BBM! 😜 *@ the creek.*

Ana:

Laur, B is ridic mean!

I grinned, deciding to go along with Ana's teasing.

Lauren:

I know, A. ☹ ☹ *How sad 4 her that she has no one 2 talk 2 . . . all alone. In the car. With her MOM.*

Ana:

Guess her Mom is her new BFF.

Lauren:

And she tells her *all her secrets.*

Brielle:

LOL. U dorks. Look up from your phones.

Huh?

I looked up. Dad had pulled the SUV to a halt in Kim's parking lot. Parked beside us was Ana. Standing in front of the cars, arms crossed and looking smug, Brielle—shaking her head, laughing.

"Oh, my God," I said, giggling. "How long have we been here?"

There was an amused smile on Dad's face. "See what happens when you text and don't pay attention? Your chauffeur has delivered you. Now get out of my car."

I couldn't stop laughing. "'Bye, Dad. Love you."

"TTYL, LT."

I rolled my eyes at him jokingly. "Thanks, Jeeves," I replied in kind. "Now run along."

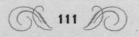

He clutched his heart. "That one hurt," he said.

"You love me," I laughed.

I got out and walked in front of the headlights to meet Brielle and Ana.

"That was pretty amazing," Brielle said. Her thick black hair was tied back with a new glittery purple headband—I made a mental note to ask her where she'd gotten it later. "When *would* you guys have stopped texting, do you think?"

Ana shot me a *go-with-me* look. "Please. Lauren and I knew exactly what we were doing. We just . . . pretended not to know we'd, you know, stopped and that you were right in front of us."

"Yeah," I jumped in. "And we got you too—ha."

Brielle stared at us and I tried to look back without squirming, but I couldn't. I was always the first one to crack.

"Okay, okay!" I said, letting out the laugh I'd been holding in.

"Laur!" Ana shook her head. "Geez. Couldn't even last ten seconds."

The three of us linked arms and made our way toward the stable. In this moment, I couldn't imagine leaving my friends, Cricket, Briar Creek, and certainly not Taylor. For the first time since she'd told me about it, I was *glad* Kim had told the Canterwood coach about my accident. Now I was prepared for the rejection. And possibly even a little relieved by it.

I walked down the aisle, passing the stalls. Some had been renovated recently and others were on the list. I examined Cricket's stall, which hadn't been redone yet. The wooden boards had been warped over the years by humidity. There were horseshoe scrapes in places where an upset horse had kicked the wood. At one time there had been a horse who'd cribbed the wood, leaving bite marks along the top of Cricket's stall door.

"Hi, girly," I said. Her gorgeous bay head poked over the stall door. She strained her neck to reach for me, and I rubbed her muzzle. What a cutie. "Let's get you tacked up so we can get to our lesson. After, we're going trail riding in the woods and we'll cool off in the creek."

When I'd first started riding Cricket, she'd *hated* trail riding. She'd wanted to stay close to the stable, fighting to go back whenever I'd take her out. But when Brielle, Ana, and I had become friends, we'd wanted to get away from the stable to talk and have fun. I'd told them how much Cricket hated the trails, but they weren't worried.

We'd gone out, and immediately Cricket had started acting up—flaring her nostrils and putting her ears back. After a few minutes she'd started to watch Breeze, who was enjoying every second of the ride. Cricket began to relax more and more each time we went out. Now I often forgot how much she'd used to hate it.

I grabbed her tack, got her groomed and ready, and, together, we headed to the indoor arena. We were the first inside.

Brielle, Ana, Leah, and Dianna trickled in as we warmed up. I had a feeling today would be a flat-work lesson. I didn't see any jumps set up. Plus, we'd jumped last time *and* Kim had given us a dressage pattern to memorize at the end of last week's lesson. I could memorize a dressage test in minutes. If only that applied to schoolwork!

We warmed up our horses by walking and trotting them in circles and figure eights. The indoor arena wasn't very big, so we had to be mindful of where everyone else was in the arena.

Kim walked inside, and I smiled when I saw what was in her hand—dressage markers.

"Leah? Ana? Would you mind dismounting and help-ing me place these?" Kim asked.

Both girls got out of their saddles and took a handful of markers from Kim. They placed them around the arena, and soon the markers, A, K, E, H, C, M, B, F, were in place in the twenty-by-forty meter pattern.

My heartbeat picked up.

This was my world. I lived and breathed dressage. I'd first seen it in the Olympics when I was five. I'd been hooked ever since.

My parents had taken me to a local show a few weeks later. I remember sneaking away from them to go down by the arena, as close as I could get, to watch. The horse and rider, so in sync, had been captivating.

"Lauren?" Kim called. "Pay attention, okay?"

"Sorry," I said. My face burned with embarrassment and I snapped out of my daydream.

She turned her gaze back to our group. "You're each going to ride the dressage pattern you've memorized," Kim continued. "I will not be calling out movements unless you get off track. Leah, I'd like you to ride first."

Leah, a fairly pretty brunette, was the least experienced dressage rider in our class, but she was learning fast.

She nodded to Kim and tightened her reins. Her Dutch Warmblood gelding, Forrest, was *huge* at almost seventeen hands high—a funny match for his petite rider—but

Leah rode him so well. The rest of us moved our horses out of the way and prepared to watch her ride.

Leah let the black gelding into a smooth walk to X. She stopped, saluting sharply, and began the pattern we'd all learned. I knew every movement, and I said them to myself as Leah rode, hoping she wouldn't go off course. Leah and Forrest had a beautiful ride—they only had a few trouble spots.

"Leah," Kim said. "That was nice. A couple of your circles were a few meters off, and I'd like you to work on cleaner transitions. Remember that they should be seamless—this requires grace. Think of dressage like a ballet. A professional ballerina does not stop between each sequence of movements. Her dance is one movement, as far as the audience is concerned. One moment she is posed in an arabesque. The next she is in the air. The transition is invisible to the naked eye."

Leah nodded. "I will. I knew our first circle was off, and then Forrest seemed to think that's what I wanted him to do for the next circle. But it was my fault for allowing him."

"I'd like you to work on those. Next lesson, I'll be looking for improvement," Kim said.

She turned to me. "Lauren, your turn."

Then a strange thing happened. The anxiety I'd been holding on to in every muscle, every bone in my body, from my other lesson—the way I'd choked before the jump. The way my stomach had fallen to my knees when Kim had told me what she'd disclosed to Canterwood about my accident. It was all gone—the bad memories, the clenched stomached feeling of failure. All of the unwanted baggage I'd been carrying around with me since the failed jump fell away from me.

I remembered who I was—the girl I'd missed so much without knowing it. Lauren Towers: competitive rider. Good at dressage. At home in the arena. I felt free.

I felt like myself again. And this was my dance.

It was me, Lauren Towers, who sank into the saddle, dropping her weight into her heels. Cricket loosened under me as she walked forward and stopped exactly on X.

I knew the four things Kim would be watching for: my position-slash-aids, Cricket's submission, her gaits, and impulsion. Ana, Brielle, and I spent hours coaching each other on all of these things. We loved that dressage's goal was to encourage a horse's athleticism and willingness to perform. I always shot for a score of sevens, with tens being the near-unobtainable best, when I rode. Today was no different.

After a salute and a brief pause, I asked Cricket to move into a trot and track left to C. We made a twenty-meter circle at E, which I could *feel* was the right size, and headed from E to K at a collected canter. I halted her at A, making her stand for five seconds, then asked her for a working trot where we made a half twenty-meter circle to the left and at C made a half twenty-meter circle to the right.

I couldn't wait to tell Cricket how well she'd done once we were back in her stall. Everything about dressage I loved. Memorizing the tests were oddly fun for me. I would draw the course with markers and read the movements to myself over and over. The circles, collected trots, extended walks, and all of the other parts that I needed in the arena were ingrained in my brain.

When I was a kid, I'd made a set of cardboard dressage markers that I'd set up in our backyard. I'd pretend I was on horseback and would "ride" the test. Sometimes I'd even put on my dressage habit—my breeches, ratcatcher blouse, stock tie, black coat, boots, and helmet.

I put my focus between Cricket's ears. The small mare liked dressage, too. We'd been a great pair because of it since I'd started riding her.

We made a couple more circles, then I eased her to a

walk and let her move into a free walk on a long rein down the center line to X. Cricket stopped, standing square, and I saluted for my final motion of the test. I joined Dianna, Leah, Brielle, and Ana.

Kim was smiling when I looked at her. "That was great, Lauren," she said. "It's evident that you're very comfortable with dressage. There's always room for improvement, but right now I'd like you to work solely on jumping before next lesson. Either in the indoor arena or with a partner outside. You've got this part. You don't need to practice as much with dressage."

"Thank you," I said. "And I will . . . do some jump work before our next lesson," I added reluctantly.

I leaned forward in the saddle to rub Cricket's neck and whisper my thanks for her incredible performance. The mare blew out a breath, most likely glad her turn was over. Now we got to relax and watch the rest of the riders.

Dianna, Brielle, and Ana had good rounds. Dianna's test was particularly sharp—every movement was alternately crisp and soft when it needed to be.

After our tests, Kim put us through a few flatwork exercises that made my legs and arms ache, but in the kind of way that I knew the workout was good for me. We worked for another half hour before Kim motioned for us to dismount. We followed her instructions and stopped our horses in front of her.

"Thank you, girls," Kim said, holding her red clip-board. "You all came prepared and worked hard. I appreciate everything you put into this lesson. We'll be working outside next class, weather permitting, so be prepared to meet in the outdoor arena. Okay! You're free to go. Have a great weekend, ladies!"

10

TRAUMA-SLASH-DRAMA

DIANNA AND LEAH WAVED TO BRIELLE, ANA, and me as they led their horses out of the arena. They were probably going shopping—it was their favorite after-lesson activity. Usually, they only stayed long enough to cool out their horses and groom them.

"Trail ride?" Ana asked, looking between me and Brielle.

I nodded. "I vote we go bareback."

"I'm in," Brielle said. "It'll keep Zane cooler."

"Same with Breeze," Ana said. "She's too hot from the lesson."

We led our horses close to the tack room, unsaddled them, and took turns holding each other's horse while we put away our saddles and pads. I brought an absorbent towel with me and the three of us dried the sweat off our horses.

Grabbing Cricket's mane in my hand, I crouched down a bit, then pushed off the ground, swinging myself onto her back.

"Show-off," Brielle said, grinning. She used the mounting block and slid onto Zane's back. Ana followed her in kind, and the three of us walked our horses out of the stable, heading for our favorite spot in the woods.

Most of the area surrounding Briar Creek was rural, so there was a ton of farmland for us to explore. Not to mention no one was ever in sight except for one elderly farmer who always refused to let us walk on his land. It was a running joke in the stable that he probably checked for hoof prints in the field every day.

I let my legs hang loose around Cricket's sides. Her ears pointed forward and there was an extra bounce in her stride as we left the stable behind—she was glad to hit the trails. Zane, Breeze, and Cricket walked side by side as we walked past the fences of the turnout pasture, another part of the Briar Creek renovation that Kim was still working on.

We kept the horses at a slow walk, making sure they

cooled and eased their muscles after the lesson. The well-worn dirt path was so familiar it was likely I'd be able to find my way to my favorite part of the trail that led to the creek with my eyes closed.

"Okay," Ana said, looking at Brielle. "So spill it already! You made us wait through the entire lesson."

"*Yeah,*" I added, having almost forgotten. "*You* IM'd *Will*! Tell!"

Brielle was one of the most popular girls in our grade and was always on dates with different guys. But she'd never like-liked any of them the way she did Will. For a second, she only smiled this *I-have-a-secret* smile.

"Bri-elle!" Ana shouted.

Brielle couldn't hold back even a second longer. "WhenIsawhimlogonIwaslikeomigod!" All of Brielle's words mashed together.

Ana and I laughed.

"Bri, if you're not into him anymore, just tell us," I teased.

Ana, known to grow impatient while popcorn was cooking in the microwave, looked like she was about to explode. "Brielle! Slow down and tell us what happened before I completely freak out."

Brielle's face was bubblegum pink. She took a breath.

"Okay. I just logged on for a second to see if I had any IMs and he logged on. I almost shut my laptop!"

"So, what'd you do?" Ana asked. The girl had zero interest in boys herself, but when it came to her BFF since kindergarten, she seemed to need to know immediately. It was adorable.

Brielle continued, her two besties hanging off of every word. "Well, I checked my messages. I mean, I wasn't going to *IM* him. I thought I heard my phone ping from a text, so I looked over to check and an IM popped up on my computer." Brielle looked at both of us, one at a time, I imagined to gauge our reactions. "It was . . . from Will," she clarified.

"We got that!" Ana exclaimed.

"What did it say?" I asked.

Brielle paused, like she was gearing up for something big. "He said 'hey, Bri.'" She squealed. "He called me Bri! Like, only you guys do that and he just *did*. I said hi and I asked him what he was doing today."

Ana, eyes wide, looked at me and we smiled at each other. Brielle was so giddy and cute about all of this.

"He said he was skateboarding with his friends. Then he asked what I was doing. I told him I had a riding lesson, then I was hanging out with you guys."

"It's a good sign that you both asked each other questions," I said. "It means he's interested in you. No doubt. Becca had told me that exact same thing when I first started IMing with Taylor."

"Well, you *might* just be right about that, LT," Brielle said. "Because he asked me to the dance!"

"What?!" Ana and I said at the same time. Our horses flicked their ears back at the noise we made.

"Brielle! This is huge!" I said.

Ana reached over and high-fived Brielle. "I'm so happy for you! We need to celebrate immediately."

"I've got to start looking for dresses and accessories, like, now," Brielle said, still smiling in a glowing-y way. "I'm going to start looking online right after this. Then I'll beg my mom to take me to the mall so I can try on options in case I order something from a Web site and it doesn't fit. I mean, it obviously has to be perfect."

"Don't worry—you're the best dress shopper I know," Ana said. "You've dragged me to the mall for, oh, I don't know, about twelve dozen shopping trips."

"We'll help you pick out *the* one," I said. "But Brielle, you're totally gorgeous no matter what you wear."

"Thanks, girls," Brielle said, the pink fading back to Bri's natural pale complexion, with a lingering happy glow.

"What would I do without you both by my side? Laur-Bell and her *killer* fashion sense and my little Ana-Banana to stay by our sides during every shopping extravaganza. *And*," she added, when Ana opened her mouth to speak, "to make sure my makeup is as stylish as a girl on a magazine cover."

Ana smiled, obviously flattered. "No artist would desert her bestie in her time of need—or, in this case, in need for makeup."

We all giggled and got the squeals and leftover questions out of our systems until the trees cleared and the dirt changed to grass.

This was one of my favorite parts of the trail because now, we had enough room to canter across the field. On the other side was the creek. I couldn't wait to take off my boots and cool my sweaty feet. If I was hot, I knew Cricket was too. The mare loved water—I had to pay attention to her every second we were wading in the creek. Once, she'd tried to lay down and roll. Bad girl.

"Let's canter," I said to my closest friends.

With collective nods as our cue, we all urged our horses into a canter. They were never competitive with each other—none of them tried to race ahead of the other. Cricket's dark mane blew in the wind, tickling my hand. I loved riding bareback.

For so long, I'd only concentrated on competing. I'd always loved horses, but not the way I did now. I paid attention to everything about Cricket, from the way she wrinkled her muzzle at smells she didn't like to the way she seemed to prance when she knew she'd done a good job at something. Riding without a saddle made me feel like part of my horse, making me that much more aware that a one-thousand-pound animal was in my hands and connected to me in the most amazing way.

Cricket took more strides than Breeze and Zane because she was smaller, but she had no problem keeping up. When her hooves struck the ground, the sound pounded in my ears. I barely moved on her back. We were completely in sync after so many lessons from Kim. Especially after our dressage practices.

Sunlight, now unfiltered from the lack of trees, hit the blades of grass, turning each blade into an emerald color. I took a deep breath of the late spring fresh air and enjoyed the way the sun warmed my face without making me feel overheated. After a few more strides, I began to pull up Cricket. Beside me, Ana and Brielle did the same.

The horses tossed their heads almost in unison, and the three of us laughed.

"We weren't the only ones who enjoyed that ride," Ana

said, patting Breeze. The strawberry roan tugged on the reins, probably sensing that the creek was near. The horses loved to play in the water as much as we did.

All three of them walked down the gentle embankment that leveled off to sandy dirt. We stayed atop our horses and tossed our boots and socks aside, then rolled up our breeches.

"Going in!" I called out, giving Cricket free rein to walk in wherever she wanted. Without hesitating, the mare stepped into the shallow part of the creek. She easily navigated around a few large rocks and struck her right foreleg against the water, sending it spraying around us.

I giggled. The cool water drops that hit my feet and legs felt good. Brielle and Ana had let Zane and Breeze into the creek. Their horses weren't timid in the water, either. Ana let Breeze stretch her neck to the water.

"Only a tiny sip for you, missy," Ana said to Breeze.

"Same for Cricket," I said. "She got colic once last year. It was so scary to go into the stall and see her trying to kick her stomach. Kim and I took turns walking Cricket for hours until her stomach felt better."

I'd hated seeing Cricket with an upset stomach.

Cricket and I waded deeper, until the water lapped at her belly. She snorted and craned her neck for a drink, then craned her neck to look at me. Water droplets on her chin hair made me laugh.

"Look, guys." I turned her toward Brielle and Ana.

"Aww!" Ana said. "She's so cute." Ana let go of Breeze's knotted reins, resting them on the mare's neck. She leaned back, resting a hand on the mare's croup. "Do you wish she was yours?"

I tilted my head. "Where did that come from?"

"Just wondering," Ana replied, shrugging. "We all ride school horses. But what if you get into Canterwood?"

I thought I saw sadness on Ana's face, but it was gone before I could be sure.

"I hadn't really thought about it," I said. "But as far as Canterwood goes, you guys know as well as I do that it's not an issue anymore. Not after Kim told the head coach about the, um, you know. Besides, the more I think about it, the happier I am that she *did* tell. About the accident, I mean. Because the more I consider it, the less I want to leave."

I smiled at my friends, but they exchanged an uneasy look.

"What?" I asked. "Did I miss something?"

"No!" They both said at once.

I raised an eyebrow.

"It's just . . . ever since you first got here," Brielle said, "Canterwood was something you always dreamed about."

I looked at Ana, watching to see what she would say.

She shrugged. "We love you, Lauren, you know we do. And if it was just the three of us—no other factors—we'd keep you here with us forever."

I smiled. I could count on Ana, she always—

"But," Ana continued, "there are *so* many other factors. Like riding. And Canterwood."

I paused, weighing my words carefully. "I get it, you guys," I said. "You're right. I always talked about getting into Canterwood."

"Dreamed about," Brielle cut in.

"True," I agreed. Beneath me, Cricket was still, as if she knew our conversation was important. "I dreamed about getting into Canterwood. I always wanted it. In fact, it's one of the reasons my family moved here. As you know, my parents told me that Sasha Silver started out at Briar Creek—that's the whole reason I wanted to be here. But things are different now."

Ana glanced at Brielle before speaking. "But," she said, "not much *has* changed. I mean, your accident—"

Brielle shot Ana a look that said *be careful!*

"I'm sorry," Ana continued. "But it's true! You wanted

to go to Canterwood long after . . . after *that*. So what else changed?"

For a second it was hard not to feel really hurt. I wanted to whirl Cricket back toward the stable. I knew I was just feeling overwhelmed by the conversation. After all, we were revisiting all of my least favorite topics to discuss these days: my accident, Canterwood, leaving all of my favorite people behind. And now, suddenly it felt like two of my favorite people were asking me to leave. Or, at least, asking an awful lot of questions about why I wasn't leaving . . . almost as if they *wanted* me to leave. I focused my gaze on Cricket for a while before I spoke. I never cried in front of anyone but my family, and I wasn't about to let that change now.

I cleared my throat, smiled, and lifted my head to make eye contact with my friends. "Okay," I said evenly. "If I felt like Canterwood was still an option, you both know me better than to think I'd turn it down"—I snapped my fingers—"just like that."

"You wouldn't?" Brielle asked.

"Of course not!" I said.

"I *told* you," Ana said to Bri, rolling her eyes. She looked at me, shaking her head. "I told Bri you wouldn't turn it down, but she didn't believe me! She was like, 'You don't know what it's like, Ana.'"

"Ana!" Bri said between her teeth.

Ana ignored her and kept talking. "She was all, 'It can be impossible to come back from getting thrown from a horse like that.' She even tried to convince me that it was hard for you to ever trust Cricket and . . . what? Why is everyone looking at me like that?"

I could feel my heartbeat rising, rising, rising so fast that it was making the collar of my shirt move with its furious, echoing beat. I realized my mouth was open in shock and I clamped it shut. My face burned—I knew it was blotchy and red.

Brielle spoke first. "Lauren, please don't be mad. It sounds awful out of context. I was so worried about you after you found out what Kim told the Canterwood coach, and you're so talented—more talented than any rider I've seen at Briar Creek. And I was so afraid you would give up. You've been through a lot—no, just please let me finish—and I was so nervous that this would be the last straw and—"

"Bri!" I finally got her to stop. I wasn't sure how long I'd been shouting her name, but it was so quiet when she'd stopped talking; even the horses seemed to have been silenced by my outburst. Not even a bird twittered.

"Bri," I continued. "I'm not mad at you. I'm not mad at anyone."

Bri started to open her mouth, then closed it. She did that a couple of times before finally saying, "You're not?"

"No," I laughed a little, my voice a bit hoarse from my mouth being open so long. "Of course not. You're right— it was hard to come back from that accident. *So* hard that I still have trouble trusting myself, let alone my horse."

Bri and Ana visibly relaxed. So did our horses."

"How could I be mad at my two besties for worrying about me? You guys are the best."

Brielle's eyes filled with tears. "Laur, I'm so relieved I—"

"Just one thing," I interrupted, holding up my hand.

"Anything," Ana squeaked so loud it was hard not to laugh.

"I need you guys to know that Canterwood has nothing to do with that stuff. Kim told them something that made it nearly impossible—that's *all*. So I'm looking on the bright side. I get to stay at a stable I love, with my family, my boyfriend, *and* my besties. That's all."

"That's all?" Brielle asked, edging Zane closer.

"Promise," I said, holding out my pinkie.

We all moved our horses closer together and linked pinkies, dissolving into giggles.

"What we said came out wrong," Brielle said. She

walked Zane into deeper water. "We would miss you so much if you went away. But I want you to—Canterwood's perfect for you, Laur. I never meant to make you feel bad. I just want you to consider it a possibility. Don't count Canterwood out just yet, that's all I ask. You're a strong candidate. I think it's still a real possibility you get in."

I knew she meant it. There wasn't an ounce of meanness in Bri.

"Okay," I said. "But if by some miracle I got it, it wouldn't be easy. I'd wish I could be in two places at once."

Ana raised a finger in the air. "I'll get right on that."

Her comment made us all smile, and the tension that had existed flowed down the creek along with the water.

I was ready for fun and to leave that heavy convo behind. Cricket, sensing my discomfort, took a step into deeper water. The fresh water hit my ankles, and it felt so good on my feet, which were terribly sore from my boots. And they were about to become even more sore soon. Last year I'd been a big-time runner. Never in competition, just for exercise around my neighborhood. I'd taken a break for a few months after my left knee had started to hurt, but it was healed now. I was ready to step into my Nikes and pound the pavement. Running was something I needed now more than ever. Aside from riding, it was my favorite way to clear my head. And obviously, I'd been away from it for too long.

But it was obvious that all three of us were ready to clear our heads and leave any more dramatic conversations for another time.

On our walk back to the stable, Ana, Brielle, and I talked and laughed about boys and school stuff until our stomachs hurt from laughter and we couldn't stop smiling if we tried.

But best of all: Canterwood hadn't come up again. Not even once.

II

SCANDAL OUTBREAK

"SHHH!"

I turned down one of Yates's many long corridors. I had minutes until first period started and I was headed to my locker.

Two girls in my grade who I barely knew had their heads together. Then, when they saw me, they only continued to stare, not talking at all.

Ohhh-kaaay. Whatever that was.

I looked away and started back toward my locker.

"That's her," someone else whispered.

I looked over and saw Sean, a guy in my history class. He was standing with one of his friends.

"Hey, what's up?" I asked, walking over to them, smiling.

Sean shrugged, pulling books out of his locker. His friend wouldn't even make eye contact with me.

"Sean? C'mon," I urged. "We're friends. Did I do something?"

Sean paused, then looked at me, "Do something? It's more like what didn't Yates do for you?"

"What? What are you talking about?"

Sean closed his locker. "Hey, you started this, not me."

He and his friend walked away without glancing my way again. I'd gotten used to Sean staring at me during history. According to Brielle, he'd had a crush on me since I'd arrived at Yates. While she thought the staring was "creepy," I'd always found him to be sweet and shy and harmless. I'd always gone out of my way to be friendly toward him. But after the way he'd just spoken to me, I thought maybe it was time to rethink the whole "friendly" thing.

This day was going from strange to just plain bizarre.

I walked to my locker, grabbed my books, and looked for Ana and Brielle. We *always* met at my locker before first period. I took out my phone, careful to keep it half-hid in my locker. Cell phones were banned at Yates and I didn't want mine to get swiped by a teacher.

Lauren:

Where r u guys?

Brielle:

Sry! We r so late. C u in class!

Lauren:

Okay.

I locked my phone. Things were so weird this morning—I really wished my besties were around for support. I *needed* them here.

I straightened my shoulders, closed my locker, and walked down the hallway. I smiled at people I knew, waiting for a smile back. But, at best, what I got in return could only be considered half smiles.

What was going on?

I got to first period and took my usual seat. I busied myself by straightening my papers and pens until I saw Brielle and Ana.

They slid into seats next to me. No one ever sat in those three seats but us.

"I'm so glad to see you guys!" I said, motioning for them to lean closer. "Everyone's being *so* weird today! I've said hi to practically everyone in school, but it's like I have the plague—people are actually going out of their way not to *look* at me, let alone speak to me."

Brielle swallowed noisily and Ana tapped her pen against her desk.

"Bri? Ana? C'mon, what's going on?" I stared at them. "You guys know and you're keeping it from me on purpose."

Ana glanced at Brielle before she looked at me. "Laur, Yates is a small school."

"Yeah?" I prodded.

Brielle broke in. "Well, small schools tend to have a lot of pride."

"Makes sense," I said, confused. "But what does this have to do with me?"

Bri went on. "Well, you're one of the most popular girls in our entire grade."

"That's not easy to do when you come in as a transfer," Ana said.

"But you did it," Brielle said, smiling. "You won over everyone at school." She paused. "But then . . . I guess people started finding out that you applied to Canterwood."

"I don't get it," I said, looking around the room at all the cold faces surrounding me. "Why do they care? I'm not even going to get in. But even if I did, this news became a scandal? *Why*?"

"I guess they care because Canterwood is Yates's biggest rival school," Ana said. "I know we don't have an equestrian team, but we do compete with them in lots of other activities like swimming, football, Scholastic Bowl . . . You applied to join the enemy school."

I felt like this had to be a dream. This was just so *juvenile*—so fifth grade! Yates was a good school—a prep school! You had to be *smart* to get into Yates. And this! "Not that I'm getting in, but it's not even like I'm interested in doing any of those things. I'm a rider, period. Yates doesn't have an equestrian team, so even if I got in, why would anyone care if I rode for Canterwood's equestrian team? How on earth did this become such a big deal?"

"Hey, it's not even worth getting upset about," Ana said, her tone soothing. "Everyone can think what they want. Who cares? We've got your back."

I smiled as best I could. "Thanks. I know you guys are on my side. It was just such a shock to come in this morning and to have everyone randomly treat me like an outcast that way. It was so . . . strange."

"Don't even react to it," Brielle said. "Stay the same fabulous Lauren you've always been. People will sniff out a bigger scandal by lunch—trust me. They'll forget all about your Canterwood application and will spend their time freezing out the next poor victim of their collective boredom."

I smiled. Brielle could always calm me down, no matter

what was going on. I wished I had her impenetrability and arid coolness.

Our history teacher, Mr. Wren, walked into the room. The three of us pulled apart, turning to the whiteboard.

I shifted in my seat, avoiding eye contact with everyone.

I was, well, used to being popular. I didn't know how to handle everyone turning on me so suddenly. Listening to Brielle and Ana was, I know, the best thing I could possibly do. Besides, they were my besties, and besties looked out for one another. Whatever I'd done to deserve such amazing friends, I was grateful.

"Morning, class," Mr. Wren boomed. "I expect you've all done the homework, so I'm going to pair you each up with a partner. One at a time, you'll come up to the board, and you and your partner will ask the class a question from the homework assignment."

I'd always liked getting up in front of the class and doing activities. I was good at it, and it made for a good grade—something that meant a lot to me.

Mr. Wren split our small class up into pairs, and I smiled when he called my name and Irina's. She was quiet and friendly, already Ivy League—college bound since she was on Yates's fast track and would probably graduate from high school a year early.

"Irina and Lauren," Mr. Wren called once he was done assigning partners. "First up."

We got up, both of us holding our homework papers. Like mine, I could see Irina's was filled—her tiny handwriting running over the margins.

We got up to the board and each uncapped dry-erase markers. "What question do you want to pose to the class?" I asked Irina.

She shrugged. "Just ask the first one and let's get this over with." Her long, almost white-blond hair fell in front of her eyes.

"Are you okay?" I whispered, genuinely confused.

"Fine," Irina said. "But why you're wasting your time coming to class and pretending to care about any of this, I don't get *at all*. But it's your life, so *what*-ever."

I shook my head. "Um, I care because I *go* here. And one day I'd like to graduate, preferably within the top five percent of my class, Irina. Please tell me you aren't mad that I applied to Canterwood, too?"

Irina's blue eyes were bored. "Not mad; over it. So, if you think you're too good for this place, which you clearly do if you're looking at Canterwood Crest Academy now, stop wasting time at Yates and go already."

Tears burned my eyes. *Stop*, I reprimanded myself. *No tears.*

"Girls, are you ready?" Mr. Wren asked.

"Yes, sir," Irina said, turning away from me. She wrote out a question for the class on the whiteboard. "We want to discuss the first question from the homework assignment," she said, suddenly upbeat.

I stood there, my face paling by the second. I knew I'd get a low participation grade, but I didn't care—I let Irina take over.

Once we were finally done, I went back to my seat. Brielle reached over to touch my arm, and I offered her the fakest *I'm totally fine!* smile I could muster.

I loved Bri for telling me to be my "fabulous" self until this blew over. Two problems: First, I had a feeling this ban on speaking to me wouldn't go away anytime soon. Second, I was feeling anything but fabulous lately.

The rest of my classes were the same.

Ana and Brielle were the only ones to talk to me nicely all day. I didn't have any classes with Taylor, but I didn't even feel like texting him to explain. Sure, he'd be mad on my behalf, but there wasn't anything he could do.

At lunch, Brielle, Ana, and I usually had to politely turn down offers to sit at half a dozen different tables. It was time we set aside for the three of us to catch up, but we always made sure not to do it in a cliquey way.

In the lunch line, I kept my eyes on the food behind the glass, hoping that my friends would be right—that something new and distracting would have turned up by now.

I ordered Greek yogurt, a veggie burger, and Pellegrino water. Then I left the safety of the lunch line and stepped into the airy cafeteria, scanning for my usual table. Brielle and Ana weren't there. For a moment, I panicked. Instinct told me to get out now. But I refused to let panic run my life. I straightened my posture and, spotting my table, decided I'd snag it for the three of us.

I walked past a bunch of tables. I couldn't decide whether to feel crushed or relieved that no one even looked up at me as I moved across the room.

"Little Miss Lauren Towers," said Hannah, a social climber who'd be friends with anyone if it got her a seat at the cool table.

At my table.

I stopped by Hannah's table. Flanked by her posse, she brushed back her dark, chemically damaged hair.

Don't stoop to her level, I admonished myself.

"So, you're too good for Yates already." Hannah said. "Did you come here just to be able to learn all about us, to turn around and whisper into the ears of *Canterwood* students?"

"Hardly, Hannah," I said. "Not that I have to explain to you or anyone else why I applied to Canterwood. And guess what? I know this may come as a shock to you, but it's not a crime to apply to other schools."

"True. Unless you're crossing into enemy territory, which you are." Hannah's dark brown eyes were smiling and suddenly, I got it.

Hannah *wanted* me to leave. Once I was gone, she'd be able to take my place on the social ladder.

Good luck getting Brielle and Ana to become your best friends, I thought. Hannah couldn't become number one without them—and Ana and Bri wouldn't let that happen. We'd become friends at the stable because we'd just clicked. I hadn't known they were the It-Girls at Yates. After all, school hadn't even started yet when we'd met. They were just two girls that I liked at the stable. The first day of school, they'd invited me to sit with them at lunch. Ever since, the three of us had been joined at the hip.

Befriending Bri and Ana had never involved popularity. To me, popularity was measured by how you treated people and, in turn, the way people saw *you*.

I continued walking, staring straight ahead, my kitten-heeled sandals clicking on the floor. Once I got to our table, my tray clattered when I set it down and my glass Pellegrino bottle almost tipped over and shattered. Suddenly, Yates didn't feel like *my* school anymore. For the first time since moving to Union, I felt like an outsider—like the new girl.

At least it was the final week of school. Maybe in the fall, when I didn't get into Canterwood, everyone would be over it by then.

But part of me, a tiny part, thought of something else: If I got into Canterwood, I'd never have to see any of them ever again.

12

HOW ABOUT A LITTLE UNDERSTANDING?

AFTER CLASS ON MONDAY, I SHUT MY BED-room door behind me and tossed my backpack onto the floor.

Ugh! I flopped onto my bed, massaging my temples with my fingers.

School hadn't gotten any better. As if things could possibly have gotten any worse, Brielle and Ana—my *best* friends—seemed to be distancing themselves from me. Since, you know, my social leprosy was contagious. I took a meditative breath. It was an hour before my riding lesson and I needed to get my mind off school so that I could put my focus where it belonged: in the arena.

Beside me, my phone chimed.

Taylor:

Hey! Didn't c u all day. U ok?

Lauren:

Yeah. Just glad school's over.

Taylor:

Laur, if ur talking abt what ppl are saying—don't let them ruin this 4 u.

Lauren:

Trying not 2. It's hard.

Taylor:

Ur stronger than this—I know it.

Lauren:

Thx. But I don't get the big deal.

Taylor:

Yates is tight. Ppl prob thnk ur leaving 4 smthng better.

Why did *everyone* keep saying that? It wasn't true and I was sick of hearing the pathetic excuse.

Lauren:

But, I'm not. You know that. I know that.

Taylor:

I know, Laur. I was only guessing what people are probably thinking. But who cares—you don't know for sure what's going on and it's the last week of school. Stick with B and A or me.

Lauren:

I will. Thanks, Tay. TTYL.

Taylor:

Laur—pls don't worry about it. Rlly. We should talk ltr.

Lauren:

Thanks. Rlly. I'm ok.

I exited our chat. It didn't feel as though my friends or my boyfriend understood what I was going through. I buried my face in my pillow, taking several deep breaths.

I thought about our Brooklyn brownstone. I needed a cup of tea.

I got up and walked to the kitchen, taking my time choosing my tea. I decided I needed something calming and without caffeine. The teapot whistled and I poured the kettle water over a vanilla chamomile tea bag. I took my time pouring, watching the tea bag drown and resurface, drown and resurface.

The house was empty—Mom was at work and Dad was picking up Becca from lacrosse practice.

I climbed into the second story bay window, warming my fingers on my blue tea mug with white daisies.

Try to put yourself in Brielle, Ana, or Taylor's position, I told myself. No matter what I'd said about being sure I'd be rejected, they all thought I might be leaving. *You'd act the same way if one of them could be leaving,* I told myself.

Was that true? Maybe. And maybe I hadn't given any

of them enough credit. Or maybe I hadn't thought enough about how hard any of this had to be on *them*.

I sipped my tea, feeling the calming liquid slide all the way down my throat, my esophagus, and finally settling in my stomach.

I had a lot of homework to do for the last week of school. But Yates teachers didn't let up for a second. Maybe, just for a minute, I needed to sit here in the quiet to enjoy my cup of tea-kettle tea.

I owed myself at least that.

POKER FACE

I RAN UP BRIAR CREEK'S DRIVEWAY ON
Wednesday at a fast clip. It was a gloomy, overcast day, and
I was already running behind. My last class had run over
because our test had begun late. Apparently, the teachers
didn't care that some of us actually had activities to get
to after school.

I slowed to a fast walk, not wanting to scare any horses
by running in the stable, and headed for the tack room.

"But Hannah wants to hang with us. She's been kiss-
ing up for days."

I stopped when I heard that from inside the tack room.
The voice was unmistakable.

Brielle.

Flattening my back against the door, I edged closer.

Eavesdropping was not my style, but this didn't sound like something they'd talked to me about.

"We *hate* Hannah," Ana said. "If Laur goes away next fall, we can't just bring Hannah into our group. You know there's only one reason why she wants to hang with us."

"To be popular," Brielle answered. "But face it, Ana. Lauren is leaving. Hannah is next in line to be most popular and she thinks she needs *us*. Wouldn't it be smart to pretend like she's right and invite her into our group so we can all just stay on top?"

There was a long pause.

I couldn't *believe* what I was hearing! If I really ever left, of course I wanted Brielle and Ana to find other friends, but not *Hannah*. I thought we'd all hated her for what she'd done to me. I mean, Ana and Brielle were my closest friends. And I was still *here*! This made zero sense.

"I like being popular," Ana said. "I guess I'd rather Hannah hang with us than to lose our place to her and the lame girls she hangs with."

"Exactly," Brielle said. "Not the best way to start seventh grade."

My stomach did a flip. Were these people really my closest friends? They sounded like strangers now—calculating and cold like every other Yates student who'd ditched me the second they found out that I'd applied to Canterwood.

I didn't want to hear another word.

I pushed the tack room door open and it banged against the wall, making a loud sound. Brielle and Ana jumped. I was glad, for once, that Kim hadn't gotten around to re-installing a new doorstop.

"What's going on?" I asked.

There hadn't even been a second when I'd thought about pretending I hadn't heard them. First, I didn't have a poker face. Second, playing games wasn't my style.

Brielle and Ana's faces turned pink. No poker faces there, either.

"Hey," Brielle said, her voice unnaturally high. "We're just getting our tack—we're late. You just get here?"

"Stop, Brielle," I said. "Just . . . stop. I heard what you just said."

"What?" Ana asked, her voice low.

"I heard all of it," I said.

"Laur," Brielle said, twisting a lock of her loose hair. "Look, we're sorry. We were just talking about possibilities. Options. Things Ana and I might need to do to keep up our status if you left next year."

"Your *status*? I haven't even gotten a *reply* from

Canterwood, let alone an acceptance." I didn't mean to yell, but my frustration with everyone and the entire situation seemed to be coming out all at once. "I can't believe you guys were my *best friends*! I had no idea I was so replaceable. Especially when *Hannah* is the one replacing me. Hannah, who humiliated me in front of the entire room just the other day."

"We're *not* replacing you," Ana said. She tried to touch my arm, but I jerked it away. "Laur-Bell, I promise. No one could ever take your place as our bestie."

"So what role will Hannah play?" I snapped.

Brielle and Ana were silent for a second.

"Hannah," Brielle finally started, "would become part of our group so that Ana and I stay popular. I mean, what if she realizes she doesn't *need* us. We're supposed to just let Hannah and her little friends take over our grade? I don't think so. We were only *considering* asking her to be friends with us so we could stay popular."

"Since when do we care that much about being popular?" I asked. "I never cared what other people thought of me until I had you guys. Being popular at Yates? It just happened. We were all nice to people and, face it, we got a little lucky. Is this what you want whether I'm here or not?"

Ana gave a small nod. "Yeah," she said.

I looked as her as though she were a stranger. And in a way, the Ana I was friends with was not the Ana before me now.

"I know, I know. I'm an artist, right? I shouldn't care what people think. I should only think about art and *feelings*. But you know what? I *like* being popular. I like my spot at the top. I want to stay there."

I stared at Ana like I'd never seen her before. "Wow," I said, unable to keep emotion out of my voice this time. My eyes filled with shock and furious tears. "I have no idea who you are, Ana."

"Lauren," Brielle said. "Please don't be upset. We were only talking about options for next year. Just like you're doing with Canterwood."

"It's not the same thing!" I shouted, stepping around them and grabbing Cricket's tack. "I applied to Canterwood to work hard and challenge myself as a rider. You guys are . . . manipulating people in order to *make* them think you're someone you're not. You're pretending to like people you can't stand—all for a spot in the freaking *lunchroom*."

I stared at them for a while, at the makeup I hadn't noticed they'd begun to wear. The expensive trendy bags with labels others coveted always promptly displayed. Clothes with skirts getting shorter and shorter, necklines inching lower. I, for the lack of anything to say, opened the tack room door to leave. And with one last, sad look, said what it was I was truly feeling to people who used to be my friends. Not popular girls, or my besties, or the people I'd once confided in. But strangers who I thought I'd known—only one short day ago.

"I hope you get what you want," I told them. "But if what you want is nothing but popularity, I feel deeply sorry for you."

I let the door swing shut behind me, leaving them in the room and glad that they didn't follow me, despite the fact they'd both called my name when I'd left.

When I got to Cricket's stall, I took her tack inside with me, picked up her grooming kit from the top of her trunk, and locked us both inside. I didn't want to be out in the aisle with everyone else. Hiding in here was impossible—Brielle and Ana would find me eventually, but at least I'd get some space from everyone else.

I busied myself grooming Cricket. The bay mare's coat was dusty from being in her stall overnight, but making it shine was easy. I whisked dirt off her back and sides. Her coat began to gleam with each brushstroke.

"At least I know you're not hoping I leave so you can find a new rider to replace me," I muttered. "Besides, the joke would be on you. I'm not getting into Canterwood, girl."

I fell into a rhythm of grooming Cricket while my thoughts wandered. Had I made a mistake just by *applying* to Canterwood? If there was this much turmoil going on before I got a yes or no, I couldn't imagine what would happen once everyone found out I hadn't gotten in. Would everyone keep hating me because I'd once tried to leave? Would I have to watch Hannah, Brielle, and Ana become the worst kind of people imaginable just to stay popular? How far would they go to hold on to their lunch table? Would I have to watch my former friends become the worst people in the world while the girls I'd once confided in disappeared, bit by bit, until there was nothing left?

Someone knocked on Cricket's stall door. I looked up at Brielle and Ana, peering at me.

"Can we come in?" Ana asked. "Just for a sec and then we'll leave."

"Sure," I said. "Do what you like."

They unlatched Cricket's stall door and closed it behind them. I refused to stop what I was doing. Cricket took the bit from my palm, and I eased the bridle over her head.

"We're both sorry you overheard that," Ana said. "If I were you, I'd never want to talk to either one of us again. I understand why you're upset and you should be. Brielle and I both made a mistake—we should have talked to you about the Hannah thing."

"I would have felt completely betrayed if I'd walked in on that conversation," Brielle said. "But beyond that, it would have felt like I couldn't trust my best friends. That would be worse than the actual conversation."

I looked at both of them. I could hear how sorry they were now, but I couldn't shake what I'd seen and heard in the tack room. Brielle and Ana had once been my support system. I'd once needed them, and when I did, they'd been there for me. I wouldn't ever forget those girls. But the girls who stood before me—they looked confused. Like they weren't sure how to quite grow up.

"I wish you guys had talked to me about this earlier," I said. "But you have to do whatever you want at school. Be friends with whomever you want. If that's Hannah, then it's Hannah."

"You have to know that Ana and I never wanted to lose *you* as a best friend. No matter where you go—or don't," Brielle said. Her eyes were wide as she looked at me. "It's hard for us, thinking about you leaving. We want to cheer you on a thousand percent—"

"You did once," I interrupted. "Both of you."

"We'll be really sad when you leave," Ana added. "We want you to go to Canterwood, and despite what you believe, we're sure you're going to get in. And then, we lose you."

Ana's dark eyes got teary.

"Guys." I stopped grooming Cricket and turned to look at them both. "Even if I did leave, you wouldn't have lost me. Besties forever, no matter where any of us are, remember? That's what we said, not too long ago."

That made both of them smile.

"We were being stupid back there about the popularity thing. We were dumb and scared about people hating us for being friends with you. About losing you to Canterwood."

I nodded, tears welling in my eyes. "It's a pretty awful feeling, seeing your best friends as strangers."

"We hated it, too," Brielle said. "We tried being those people for a little while. They were kind of jerks."

I nodded. "Kind of?" I asked.

It had been a while since I'd laughed.

Ana and Brielle laughed, too.

"They were *really* awful," Ana said. She smiled, despite the tears rolling down her face.

Will we be okay?" Ana asked, giving me a tentative smile.

"We might be," I said. "Someday. But now we have to go explain to Kim why we just missed our entire lesson."

Together, we left Cricket's stall.

14

I'VE GOT MAIL

AFTER SCHOOL, I CLIMBED OUT OF MY DAD'S SUV.

One more day left! Thursday was finally over, which meant that finals were done.

Friday would be a completely random day. We had to clean out our desks and lockers, get summer reading and homework assignments, and *our* class got to have a pizza party at the end of the day because we'd all gotten good grades this year. Like anyone at Yates got bad grades!

People at school had been so wrapped up in finals and celebrating the end of the school year that no one paid any attention to me or the fact that I'd become a traitor outcast overnight.

Taylor had texted me after his last final, and he'd been beyond excited.

Taylor:

Duuude! Finals r over!!!

Lauren:

Do you believe it?!☺ ☺ We made it! Hello, 7ᵗʰ grade!

Taylor:

We'll have 2 celebrate extra @ the dance.

Lauren:

Sounds like a date!

Just thinking about our chat made me smile. Friday night's dance was exactly what I needed—time to have fun and wash the last horrible week of school away. It still wasn't sinking in that sixth grade was one day away from being over.

"I'm going to check the mail," I told Dad.

"Okay, hon." He took my heavy book bag from me and I walked down the driveway, taking my time.

I pulled my Chanel sunglasses, a gift from my Manhattan financier aunt, over my eyes and let the warm sunlight bathe my pale face.

I took off my cream-colored three-quarter sleeve knit cardigan, revealing my lacey yellow tank. I'd have to load up on the sunscreen today—good as it felt, my ridiculously fair skin was already getting pink from ten seconds in the sun.

Our mailbox was stuffed with the usual—*The New Yorker* (Mom), *Sports Illustrated* (Dad), *TeenStyle* (me and Becca), bills, and junk mail.

I wasn't disappointed. I'd given up on waiting for a letter from Canterwood Crest Academy. I realized they'd probably already sent their acceptance letters to new students. The rejections would most likely trickle in later. I shifted the mail to my other arm. Dad's *Sports Illustrated* slipped out of my hands and, grumbling to myself, I bent over to pick it up.

Apparently, I'd dropped more than just one magazine, too. I blamed it on the sun. It had been so long since it had shown its face in Union, it was throwing me off. I looked down at the magazine, a couple of bills, and some junk-mail envelopes.

"Geez, Lauren!" I scolded myself. As I was gathering up the mail, I saw it.

It was heavy and creamy with a thick, expensive-feeling texture. Like one of those *"You've won a trip to the Caribbean!"* letters. It was facedown on the ground.

As if the envelope contained toxic material, I flipped it over onto the sidewalk with one finger. My eyes went right to the return address. It almost made my heart stop.

CANTERWOOD CREST ACADEMY

Why was it so big? Everyone knew rejection letters were small—just simple, letter-sized envelopes. Unless . . . unless it was a super-fancy rejection. I mean, Canterwood was one of the most exclusive boarding schools in the country. Maybe they spared no expense—even for the losers.

I wished my heard would stop pounding—it was tricking my brain! The last thing I needed right now was to undo *months* of preparation. I'd finally convinced myself— and everyone around me—that there was no chance for me at Canterwood. Well, except for Brielle and Ana, they'd never believed I wasn't getting in, but that was just them.

Oh, and Taylor. But he was just being supportive. Plus, he was a swimmer. He didn't know that kind of accident I'd had was a career-killer for equestrians once people found out. I mean, everyone knew that.

Except for Becca, of course. She was just trying to spare my feelings, though, telling me that mistakes like that only made me a better rider. But she was my *sister*. What else was she going to say? "You're doomed forever, have a great life?"

And, of course, my parents were similarly supportive. Who told their own children they were destined for certain rejection for the rest of their lives?

Okay, so those were all the people I was close to. So what? Who knew my own destiny better than *me*?

Thump thump thumpthumpthumpthump! Stupid heart!

I sighed and stood up, leaving the envelope on the driveway. The only way to find out was to pick it up. But . . . this was ridiculous. My future was sort of in there, on the ground. I'd either be Lauren Towers, enrolling at Canterwood, or I'd (more likely) be Lauren Towers, going back to Yates.

I stared at the envelope for at least five more minutes before I picked it up, holding it between two fingers.

Just take it inside and open it with Mom and Dad, I told myself. I wanted their support when I opened it. Not that I needed support. I mean, Yates was a far cry from a life sentence in juvie. Either way, I'd be happy.

Still, I walked at a snail's pace up the winding driveway. I reached the porch steps and stopped.

This was something I wanted to do on my own. It always had been. So what was I waiting for?

I sat down and dropped the rest of the mail beside me. My fingers were shaking so much (Why? Hadn't I just spent months convincing myself that I was better off here in Union?) that I almost gave myself a paper cut opening the envelope. The gold lining in the envelope reflected against the sunlight.

I froze. I couldn't. Everything was going to change (no matter what the outcome) the second I opened the letter, and there was no way around that fact. No way to convince myself otherwise.

Squeezing my eyes shut, I pulled the letter out of the envelope and unfolded it. Peeking between the fingers of my right hand, I looked at the letter.

```
          Canterwood Crest Academy
              107 Greenwich Drive
          East Brookfield, Connecticut


    Lauren Towers                May 16th
    28 Dalton Road
    Union, Connecticut


    Dear Ms. Towers:
    Thank you for your application
    to Canterwood Crest Academy. As
    you are well aware, our world-
```

renowned Academy receives thousands
of applications from talented
students across the country and
internationally. This year's
application pool for fall was
exceptionally strong.

We have carefully reviewed
your information and have given
considerable thought to the
possibility of your future as a
student at Canterwood Crest Academy.
This process is one which we at the
Academy do not take lightly. Our
students are the best and brightest
in the nation—many of whom have
gone on to become doctors, lawyers,
Olympians, and future leaders of our
country. Many have won prestigious
awards, such as the Pulitzer and the
Nobel Peace Prize, not to mention
numerous national awards within
our graduates' chosen fields of
practice.

Acceptance to Canterwood Crest
Academy is not only an honor, it is a
symbol of each candidate's potential
to become one of the greatest
students, most successful athletes,
and most prestigious scholars.

It is with great pleasure that we are
offering you a spot this fall.

To those who have been accepted,
we would be honored to have you
in attendance. You have already
attained a goal that most are not
considered talented enough to attain.
Congratulations on taking the first
step on your journey toward becoming
one of the most sought-after scholars
in the nation. Your journey has only
just begun, and your acceptance is
only the beginning of your future as
a role model and leader.

Please let us know at your earliest

convenience of your decision, and we
look forward to hearing from you.

Sincerely,
Headmistress Drake

I read the words over and over until they melted together.

"No! No way! Omigod—it's not, it's—omigod!" I screamed, clutching the letter as I jumped up.

I left the rest of the mail on the porch and turned toward the door.

I had to tell Mom and Dad! And—oh, Becca!

After minutes of shock it hit me all at once at full force—I'd been chosen.

15

IN

"MOM, DAD!" I CALLED WHEN I GOT INSIDE. "Mom!"

"Lauren, what's wrong?" Mom said, hurrying from her office.

Dad appeared right behind her, his eyes wide. "Are you okay?" he asked.

"I got it! I got it!" I screamed, probably rattling the windows in the house.

"Got what? Lauren!" Mom reached for my hand that was waving the envelope in the air. She plucked it from my hand, saw the letter, and scanned it speed-reader-lawyer style.

"Oh, Lauren!" Mom dropped the letter on the foyer table and ran over to grab me and wrap me up in a hug.

"I'm *in*! I squealed." I'm going to Canterwood!"

"I knew it!" Dad swooped me off the ground and twirled me around like I was five again. "I'm so proud of my little Laur-Bell. Oh, honey. You did it! You're in!"

I was laughing—and dizzy—when he set me down.

"Lauren, come into the kitchen," Mom said. "Let me make you some lemonade. You must be thirsty from all that screaming."

I laughed. "Thanks, Mom. There's so much to do. Omigosh—I have to tell people. Taylor, maybe even Ana and Brielle. . . . Can I go call all of my friends after?"

"Of course you can," Mom said. "I'm going to call Grandma and Grandpa. They'll be so happy for you."

I took a sip of my mother's fresh-squeezed lemonade, the glass rimmed with sugar.

"Yum, Mom. Thank you," I said.

"You're welcome," Mom said. "And think about where you want to go for dinner tonight—it's *your* choice."

I got up from the table, grinning, and with my lemonade in hand took the stairs two at a time to my room. I was bummed that Becca wasn't home—she was out with her boyfriend. But there was no way I'd tell her via text; I'd wait until she got home.

I opened BBM and scrolled to my group chat with Brielle and Ana.

Lauren:

Can u guys talk?

The wait, even though it was only seconds, felt excruciating. After our last conversation, I didn't know *how* this one would go, but I had to tell them. I just had to.

Brielle:

Laur?! Totally! Call me!

Ana:

Me too!

Lauren:

Okay—calling u guys now.

I got them on conference call. It was better just to get it over with. *Tell them right away*, I told myself.

"So what's going on?" Brielle asked. "Are you okay?"

"Yeah," Ana said. "You scared me—I thought something bad happened."

"Sorry. I mean, it's not bad news. Not even close. Guys, I . . ."

I didn't know how to tell them. I froze. Was I supposed to sound elated that I was going to Canterwood, which meant I was leaving them *and* Yates, especially after the weirdness that had passed between us at practice? Or was I supposed to sound excited but a little sad?

Just be honest and say how you feel, I decided. *They have been your best friends for a year and a half. They're going to be happy if you are, no matter what happened at practice.* "Laur?" Bri and Ana said at the same time.

"I . . . I got my letter from Canterwood just a few minutes ago."

There was silence on the other lines.

Just say it.

"I got in."

"LAUREN!" Brielle and Ana screamed into the phone at the same time.

Giggling, I held it away from my ear while they shrieked. Relief at their reactions made my palms stop sweating.

"I totally knew it!" Ana said. "You were in from the second you applied."

"*So* in," Brielle added. "You're going to *Canterwood*! To boarding school!"

I tried not to read into her "boarding school" comment. Canterwood *was* a boarding school, after all.

"I know." I shifted in my window nook. "I can't believe it. I'd been away from home a lot back when I was on the show circuit. But . . . this is permanent. I'll only be coming back home for holidays and breaks."

The thought made my heart beat a little faster. I couldn't help but wonder if I'd see Ana and Brielle over breaks or if they'd be attached to Hannah.

"But there *are* tons of holidays," Ana put in. "And you won't be *too* far away. On some of *our* days off, you know Brielle and I are totally going to crash your dorm room and visit."

"Really?" I asked, surprised.

"Of course," Brielle said. She sounded earnest. "This is your shot, Lauren. We know you can't pass it up. We're going to IM and Skype every day. You'll see more of us from Canterwood than you do here."

"Thanks, guys. That's really good to hear," I said. "It was a little hard to tell you. I wasn't sure how you'd feel. *But.* We are besties. Nothing dumb like distance is going to change what we shared in the past."

"It *is* sad," Ana said. "We'll miss you, obviously. But it would have been way more sad for all of us if you hadn't gotten in. We know you're going to do great, Laur."

"Thanks," I said, taken aback by Ana's sudden maturity.

"This is a huge deal. Celebration huge," Brielle said. "So I say we have a giant sleepover weekend this summer."

"Brielle," Ana said. "is totally right. You *better* free up your time."

I laughed. "I think I can squeeze you guys in. Maybe."

After we hung up and I put my phone down, I hugged my knees to my chest. I couldn't stop the slow smile that spread across my face.

I'm going to Canterwood.

I stared out the window at the lawn. This time next year, I wouldn't be sitting here. I'd be looking out another window, hours away, at a place I'd only seen in a virtual tour online.

Then reality hit me: Going to Canterwood meant everything was going to change.

Everything.

I was leaving Yates—a school I loved. Where up until I'd applied to Canterwood I'd fit in spectacularly well. Becca, Mom, and Dad would go on with their daily routine that I knew by heart, except I wouldn't be here. Charlotte, who was coming home from college next week, would be home all summer and then we'd *both* be leaving in the fall. I forced myself to take a breath and a gulp of lemonade. My cheeks were suddenly burning.

You're not leaving right this second, I told myself. *You'll be here all summer and a few weeks of fall.*

There was plenty of time to prepare and do the thing that always made me feel better—make lists of things I needed to do. Lists always calmed me. I had them all over my room—on my whiteboard, my computer, and on sticky notes on my door. Dad teased me that one day I was going to write "make a list" on one of my already existing lists.

The sun was starting to sink a little, an orange and yellow ball that was already half-hidden behind the trees in our backyard.

I picked up my phone and lemonade and slid my feet into white flip-flops. I walked downstairs and out the back door, bypassing the pool and going deeper into the backyard, to the hammock. It was my secret spot that I went to whenever I wanted to get out of the house and make private phone calls.

I loved the sun. Summer was my favorite season. I loved everything about it—especially fashion. Flip-flops, skirts, tank tops, and scented body sprays that smelled like summer fruits—grapefruit, sugar-peach, plum passion.

I climbed into the hammock and set my lemonade down on the plastic outdoor table. I stretched out, my fingers hovering over the speed-dial button for Taylor. I had to get it over with. I knew he'd be happy for me, but I wanted to tell him that this was something I wanted to talk about in person. He was my boyfriend. My decision to go to Canterwood would change everything for us.

Before I could sit there any longer, I pressed the three button.

"Hey," Taylor said.

"Hi." I heard papers shuffling in the background. "Are you busy?"

"For you," Taylor said. "Never too busy. I was just tossing a bunch of stuff from school that I didn't need. I can't believe tomorrow's really our last day. Can you?"

"No! This year went by so fast. We were the little kid sixth-graders and now we're almost seventh-graders."

"I know. I'm so glad classes are over. Summer break is going to be awesome. We can go out whenever we want. I already asked my parents about getting my curfew extended so I don't have to be home before dark." Taylor laughed.

"No kidding. We've got months to do whatever we want. All I want to do *is* hang out with you, maybe see Brielle and Ana—try that out again and see how it goes—and ride. No staying up until one to finish a paper for history, or spending all weekend doing a science project."

"As if we're going to need to know the parts of a cell when we graduate," Taylor said. I couldn't see him, but I knew him well enough to know he was rolling his eyes.

"Right," I said, shaking my head. "Or memorizing

lines from ancient poems that I can't even understand. I admit that I like *some* poetry, but the stuff we read in my English class this year? We spent six weeks reading these crazy poems that you had to google to even understand."

I was stalling. I admit it.

"My brain's going to explode if we talk about school for another second," Taylor said. "Change the subject. Please!"

"Well, actually I called because I have something to tell you."

"What's up?"

All of Taylor's attention was on me. That was one of the things I loved about him—he was a great listener.

"I wanted to tell you in person, but I couldn't wait until school tomorrow. So . . . I got a letter from Canterwood today."

"Lauren. You've been waiting for that forever! What did it say?"

"I can't believe it, but—" I paused, nervous. "I got in, Taylor."

"I knew it! I wish I was there to kiss you right now. I'm so proud of you, Lauren!"

He *was* proud, too. I could tell it wasn't just words. I knew he'd be happy for me—it had been my own nerves that had gotten in the way of thinking he'd be anything but happy for me.

"I can't wait to see you at the dance tomorrow night," Taylor said. "There's so much we need to talk about and celebrate."

With everything that had been going on, I'd honestly forgotten about the dance. I didn't even have a dress!

"I'm excited, too. And I definitely want to talk, Taylor. I know this doesn't just affect me, so please don't think that I'm not thinking about that or ignoring the fact that you're involved, too."

"I never thought that, Laur-Bell. We're going to sit down and figure this out together—however we have to do it. Don't worry."

"Okay."

I heard someone calling Taylor in the background.

"I've got to go," he said. "Mom needs me to help unload groceries."

"I'll BBM you later," I said.

"And Lauren? Congratulations. I'm really, really proud of you."

We hung up and I put the phone on my chest. I stayed in the hammock until dusk. It was *très parfait* out here.

Taylor's words rolled around in my head, especially "however we have to do it." The backyard started to glow with blinking fireflies while I tried to dissect what he'd meant. I was sure he meant figure out how our long-distance relationship would work.

But what if he wanted to break up?

I suddenly felt heavy, like the hammock would break under my weight. I hadn't even had time to think that far ahead—about my future with Taylor. I was so certain I wouldn't get in. I knew *I* wanted to stay together, but he had to want that too. Not that he had given me any indication that he didn't want to. I was sure I'd read too much into what he'd said.

Stop.

Just enjoy the moment, I told myself. I'd just been accepted to my dream school! Taylor and I would figure out where we'd go from here when we were face-to-face.

A few dark, puffy clouds started to roll over me and thunder boomed miles away. I loved storms. Usually I sat in the window, watching while I drank a cup of tea or did homework or read.

This time I stayed in the hammock until the rain splattered against the deck and soaked through my clothes, my hair, and ran over my skin.

Sitting in the hammock, drenched in rainwater and

thinking about my shiny new future, all I could do was smile and think about the new me: Lauren Towers, Canterwood Crest Academy *étudiante* (aka student).

I got up from the hammock, heading for the laundry room to leave my wet clothes. I changed, and with my hair still wet, went looking for Mom and Dad. There was someone I couldn't tell over the phone. Someone who had been the reason why I'd been accepted.

My parents were in the living room, their address books on the coffee table and phones in hand.

"We're still calling friends and family," Mom said. "Grandma and Grandpa are so excited for you, sweetie. They can't wait to talk with you later."

I smiled. "I can't wait to tell them about Canterwood. But there's someone I want to tell in person."

They knew before I said her name.

"I'll get my keys," Dad said.

When we reached Briar Creek, I was relieved to see the lights on in the stable. I hadn't called first, but I knew Kim would be at the stable. She was there late every night.

"I'll be just a minute," I told Dad, opening the car door.

"Take your time," he said.

The rain had stopped, and I walked through the muggy air into the stable. It was quiet except for the occasional snort or stomp from a horse. I walked down the aisle to the hallway outside Kim's office. Her door was open and she was writing in a ledger.

"Hi, Kim," I said, my voice soft.

"Lauren." Kim looked up from a stack of paperwork. She had one pen in her hand and one stuck behind her ear. "Is everything okay? I didn't know you were coming." She motioned for me to sit. I stepped into her office and sat in a red chair opposite her.

"Everything's *more* than okay," I said.

Kim smiled. "What's going on, missy? I can see it in your face that something's up."

"I . . . I checked the mail when I got home from school," I said. Every word spilled out faster than the last, leaving me almost breathless. "And there was nothing. I mean, there was junk mail. And bills. And magazines. And I dropped Dad's *Sports Illustrated*. I picked it up and I saw *it*."

Kim bit back a grin. "And what might 'it' be?"

"A letter. From Canterwood. I was so scared to open it. I was sure, so sure I wasn't getting in." My words slowed as I got myself together. "I wasn't going to even open it right away. But I did."

"And?" Kim asked, but there was an I-already-know tone to her voice.

"I got in," I whispered. "Canterwood said yes."

"Lauren! Congratulations!"

Kim got up, walked around her desk and hugged me. When she let me go and I sat back down, I felt like I'd finished a marathon. There was no way I would have been able to wait a day to tell Kim.

"I knew you'd get in, sweetie," Kim said. "You were an ideal candidate from the second you applied."

I leaned back in my chair. "I definitely didn't know. I was sure Canterwood would take one look at my application, see my accident, and toss my papers in the trash. I didn't think I was good enough."

"Laur, the accident doesn't define you," Kim said. "You're more than what happened. You're a bright, talented rider and a great student. Any school would be lucky to have you—now Canterwood will be."

I looked at Kim, thinking how devastated I'd been when she'd told me that Canterwood knew about my accident. That she'd told them. I'd been sure Kim had sealed my fate. And she had—she'd secured me a *yes*.

"Thank you," I said. "For everything. I wouldn't have gotten in without your letter of recommendation or all of the hours you've worked with me. I love riding again because of you and Briar Creek."

Kim's smile couldn't have been any bigger. "You're welcome. But don't take credit away from yourself. Canterwood accepted *you*—not my letter."

In the office light, something caught my eye.

Sasha's trophy.

"I can't believe I'm going to school with *Sasha Silver*," I said. "I want to meet her the second I get on campus. But I'm also . . . kind of scared to meet her."

Kim shook her head. "Don't be scared. Sasha will be excited to have a Briar Creek girl at Canterwood."

"I hope so," I said, glancing at the photo of the pretty girl on her chestnut horse. "I don't want her to think I'm replacing her as Union's transfer."

"There's plenty of room for two Briar Creek riders," Kim said. "You'll see."

I looked away from Sasha's photo with a grateful smile at Kim. No matter what she said, I couldn't have done it without her. And I had to make sure once I was at Canterwood that I made Kim and Briar Creek proud.

16

SOME PEOPLE WILL BEG FOR FASHION TIPS

FRIDAY WAS INSANE.

Huge trash cans were everywhere. Lockers were open and students tossed papers, pens, pretty much *anything* they didn't want to take home. I sidestepped an eighth grade boy who was tossing gray (I swear they were once white) gym socks into the trash can.

Très disgusting!

We didn't need anything for homeroom today, so I walked straight to class. I could hear the roar of summer vacay mania inside before I even opened the glass door.

Inside, everyone was talking about what they were doing over summer break. I walked by a girl who usually sat next to me in math class.

"Hi, Elizabeth," I said. "A little chaotic, no?"

"It's like Animal Planet," she grumbled.

"Got any plans for break?" I asked.

"Yeah." She shrugged, leaning back in her seat. "But why do you care?"

"What?" I said, caught off guard. "All I did was ask what you were doing this summer—what's wrong?"

Elizabeth rolled her eyes. "It doesn't matter if I tell you I'm going to Cape Cod or the moon. You're going to *Canterwood*. It's not like you're going to ask if my summer was good or not this fall. Why bother?"

I *hated* this! Everyone was being totally ridiculous. I couldn't believe they were shutting me out just for changing schools. That had never happened to me anywhere else before. Whenever I'd left, the teachers always threw a little good-bye party and everyone had promised to stay in touch.

But that never happened, I thought.

"Whatever. I'm not sorry that I'm transferring—even if it *is* to the 'enemy' school. I thought we were friends. Forgive me if I thought you were better than this. Enjoy your life, Elizabeth!"

Before she could say another word, I walked to my desk.

We'd all been told to come to homeroom first, and *then* we'd be allowed, a few at a time, to go clean out our lockers and return our books to our teachers. No one spoke to me while I waited for Brielle and Ana. Everyone was talking to someone else about summer plans, except for me. I guessed I should have realized that, at a school as competitive as Yates, students just didn't come and go. School pride definitely ran deep.

"Hi, everyone," Ms. Merner said.

She was one of my favorite teachers, and she was the only one who didn't care if we got to class two minutes late. Probably why Brielle and Ana, who slid in behind her, loved the class so much.

"Well all, your sixth-grade year is officially over," she continued. "You've all done exceptionally well and you should be proud of yourselves for everything you've accomplished this year." Ms. Merner smiled. "I enjoyed having each of you in my class. I hope you have a wonderful summer break—you've earned it. I'll see you, refreshed and ready to learn, in the fall."

The class laughed and groaned at the same time.

She laughed, too, and put a thick stack of stapled papers on the table in the front of the room.

"Speaking of refreshed," Ms. Merner said with a smile. "Each of you needs to take a packet. It contains the summer homework assignments from all of your teachers."

This time, the class only groaned.

Ms. Merner laughed harder this time, holding up her hands defensively. "Sorry, sorry! Just think of it as a way to keep your minds sharp."

More groaning.

"The first three rows can come up now, take a packet, and then go clean out your lockers," Ms. Merner said. "Whenever someone comes back, I'll send another student out."

Brielle, Ana, and I got up from our spots in the third row, our backpacks over our shoulders. I followed them up to the table, reaching for the papers, but pulled my hand away when I realized I didn't need one. I'd be doing Canterwood homework this summer.

Ana saw my mistake and turned to me, frowning. "Boo," she said. "Brielle and I won't be able to call you for answers this summer."

I smiled. "Aww, I guess you'll have to do your own work this year. Or maybe Brielle will get the answers from Will." I said his name in a teasing, singsong way.

Brielle whipped around, her hair getting stuck to her gloss. "Did you say 'Will'? What about him?"

Ana and I laughed as we left the classroom.

"You have quite the Will-dar," I giggled. "I just said

that you'd have to get homework answers from Will this summer."

Brielle nodded. "Duh. I pick smart-slash-hot guys for *a reason.*"

"You know, things got so crazy this week, I don't even have a dress for the dance tonight," I said. "Where did you get yours, Bri? And what's it look like? You haven't said a word about it."

"Shop without you? Not a chance," Brielle said. "Like I'd pick out a dress without my fashion fairy godmother. Ana and I didn't want to bug you about a dance after how awful we were to you." She bowed her head, looking guilty. "But if you're dress-less too, want to hit the mall after school? My mom can take us."

"I am definitely sans dress," I said slowly, unsure of whether I felt like we were cool enough to shop together quite yet. "But . . ."

"I know we were harsh before," Ana cut in. "But Bri might never get over it if we miss our last chance to go school dress shopping with our most fashionable bestie."

I looked in her eyes. There was no hint of fakeness in them.

"Please, please, please," Brielle said.

"What about Hannah?" I asked pointedly, raising my eyebrows.

Brielle and Ana both paled.

"Lauren, we were *such* jerks," Brielle said.

"Totally idiots," Ana confirmed.

"Let us prove it to you," Bri said. "I'm actually begging you here."

I looked at her. Bri did *not* do *faux*-begging. She meant it.

I pulled out my phone and covertly typed a quick message.

Hey Dad—I forgot 2 get a dress 4 2nite. Can I go 2 the mall w B and A after school?

Before we'd even reached our lockers, he'd written me back.

Sure, sweetie. Use the emergency credit card and call if you're going to be late.

"Okay," I said. "I'll go. But *only* because I'm afraid of what you'd show up wearing without my advice." I smiled, making sure she knew I was kidding.

"Really?!" Bri yelped.

I nodded.

"This is going to be epic!" Ana said.

Ana and Bri texted their parents to ask their permission.

Within ten minutes, we had a ride to and from the mall, and permission from all of our parents to go.

"You guys are sooo getting me Pinkberry, though, because I know we're going to be at the mall until it closes," I said.

"Deal," Brielle and Ana said at the same time.

We giggled and opened our lockers. I put my bag down, deciding to take my locker decorations down first. Carefully, I peeled off the small, heart-shaped mirrors from Pottery Barn Teen. They fit into the zipper pocket of my big backpack.

Next, I took down the photos I'd taped up of Brielle, Ana, and me. Each one made me smile. There was one of all three of us on horseback, grinning at Kim, who'd snapped the photo.

Another was of Ana at her surprise twelfth birthday party. I'd taken it when Ana had walked through her front door and we, along with a few of our other friends, jumped up from behind her living room furniture, yelling *SURPRISE!* Ana had been so shocked, she'd almost fallen backward through the doorway.

The last photo was one Ana had taken of Brielle and me with our arms around each other's shoulders. We had sunglasses on and were posing for the camera with our lips pursed—like we were posing for *Us Weekly* instead of Ana.

With a twinge of sadness and nostalgia, I put the photos in an empty folder so they wouldn't get bent. This was already harder than I'd expected. I'd tried, earlier, to pretend that I wasn't leaving Yates forever so I could get through the day without feeling any sadness. But with each moment that passed, it became more and more real that I wasn't coming back.

Ever.

"Hey," Brielle said softly. She peered around my locker door, watching me. "We're going to make sure those are framed for your dorm room at Canterwood. You know, so you can remember how gorgeous your friends at Yates are."

I blinked, determined not to break my no-crying-in-public rule. I managed to blink the tears away, but my smile was still shaky.

"We're going to clean out our lockers, return the books that made our backs hurt all year long, and then it's class party time," Ana said, lightening the mood. "And then, best of all?"

"Dress shopping!" I said. "Talk about last minute."

Brielle snorted from her locker. "Puh-lease. We'd look

awesome in anything. With you and all your fashion knowledge, I don't have any doubts we'll find something perfect."

"Is Will excited?" I asked, taking off my book covers.

"He's trying to act like a guy—not *too* excited, but happy to go with me." Brielle said. "But I can tell he's as excited as I am."

"I'm sure he is," I said. "If only guys would just be, you know, *honest* about how they're feeling about stuff."

"No kidding," Brielle said.

"That's why I'm glad I'm not going with anyone," Ana said. "I get to skip trying on a bazillion dresses, I don't have to worry about my date's feelings, and, most important, I don't have to dance unless I want to."

Brielle walked around us to carry an armful of paperwork to the trash. "Let's see if you still feel that way next year."

Ana glared playfully at her.

I pulled off all of my stretchy reusable book covers and put them in my bag. I stacked my books into a neat pile on the floor, took off my locker lock, and dropped it into my bag. A few stray pens and highlighters that had been lost all year rolled around in the bottom of my locker. I tossed them—they'd all dried up from not being used.

My locker was empty.

I stared at the blue metal, took a quiet breath, and closed the door.

The last day went by quickly. After my entire class had finished cleaning their lockers, we watched a newly released comedy in homeroom and ate Domino's pizza with soda. I'd only seen Taylor briefly today—he'd been on the way to the gym with guys from his swim team. He'd said hi and I could tell he'd wanted to talk more, but it wasn't the time. We'd talk tonight at the dance.

When the movie credits rolled, I got up with the rest of the class.

"I hope you all had fun on your last day," Ms. Merner said. "Once you gather all of your belongings, you may leave. Have a fantastic summer, everyone! See you all next year."

I realized I wasn't part of that "all." Not anymore.

I'd never seen the class move so quickly. The exit was a flurry of activity as everyone grabbed their bags and bolted out the door.

I waved to Ms. Merner as I passed her desk.

"Lauren," she said. "You've been a wonderful student to have in class. I know you'll excel at Canterwood. Good luck, and feel free to come by and visit whenever you have time off."

"Thank you," I said, beaming.

I hoped she was right about excelling at Canterwood. And the idea that I could come back to Yates and visit somehow made me feel infinitely better all of a sudden.

It made walking out of Yates—my school—for the last time easier. The day had been bittersweet, but there was one thing that made me feel absolutely elated. . . .

I was *officially* a Canterwood student now.

17
THE DRESS

"HOW LONG DO YOU THINK THIS WILL TAKE?" Ana asked that question every single time we stepped inside the mall.

"Focus on Pinkberry at the end of the tunnel," Brielle said. "Besides, it can't take too long—we have to save enough time to go home, get ready, and make our fabulous, fashionably late appearance at the dance."

"At least we didn't have a full day of school," I said. "Or we'd really have to rush."

"We'd be going in dresses from *last season*," Brielle said, making a face like she'd just had a gross bite of sashimi.

Ana and Brielle motioned for me to lead the way. I went straight for our favorite dress shop. Bella's Boutique was a local boutique-type store. It wasn't huge, so it didn't have a *ton* of options, but what they did have was unique. Not many girls in our class shopped there. They flocked to the usual chain stores and bought dresses with expensive chi-chi labels that at least three girls in various grades showed up in. Brielle and I'd always had good luck with dresses whenever we'd shopped at Bella's Boutique.

A salesclerk welcomed us.

As we walked in, I realized I hadn't been here in a while. I'd missed shopping here. I loved everything about the place. It smelled like the caramel and vanilla candles that dotted several shelves throughout the store. There were always fresh, seasonal flowers on the counter (white tulips today), and none of the store's employees followed younger shoppers around as if we were likely to steal something. The boutique also had a fun assortment of locally made jewelry that sparkled in the track lighting. It was *so* easy to accessorize and buy your dress—plus, maybe buy some irresistible-smelling lotions to make a girl feel even more gorgeous.

"Omigod," Brielle breathed.

I looked away from the jewelry and laughed. Brielle already had three dresses over her arm. Ana, smiling, reached out and took them from Brielle.

"Go ahead," Ana said. "Load me up."

Grinning, Brielle tugged on Ana's arm. "Well, if you're offering . . ."

"Before I leave you to find my own dress, B, I want to assess your dress sitch." I looked her over carefully. "So far this school year, you've worn a yellow dress and a black dress—both great for your coloring. With your dark hair and fair complexion, I vote you look for either light purple or silver, preferably form fitting, and . . ." I walked a circle around her. "Simple. I love strapless, spaghetti strap, or halter on you. Kitten heels for sure."

Brielle sighed. "What will I do when you're gone?" she asked.

"Ever hear of online shopping and a little thing called *e-mail*?" I laughed, leaving a very relieved-looking Brielle to browse so I could do the same.

I walked over to a rack of dresses and looked through them. I already knew I didn't want anything in a print. Nothing pink or purple. I'd worn both colors to other dances earlier this year. Out of the corner of my eye, I caught a swatch of ice-blue material. I walked over and lifted it off the rack.

"No way," I whispered.

The first dress I'd picked up was *it*. I knew I didn't have to look at any other dresses. This one was *the* one.

It was a slim-fitting, sleeveless dress with a sweetheart neckline. I held it up, and it skimmed a few inches above my knees. *Parfait!* With my silver ballet flats, it would be lovely. The size was exactly right for me.

I inspected the pale blue material. It was raw silk and, in the right light, had a silvery sheen that shone brilliant, like the shadow of a full, blue moon.

"Guys." I walked over to Brielle and Ana. "Look!" I held the dress up over my body and they both smiled.

"Wow. Laur, that's going to look amazing on you," Brielle said. "You found that so fast!" She turned to Ana. "She's got paranormal abilities when it comes to fashion, I'm telling you."

Ana shifted Brielle's half a dozen dresses in her arms. "Love it. Go try it on!"

"Okay! Be right back." After promising Bri I'd help her when I was out, I headed for the dressing room. Locking the door behind me, I put my backpack down and slipped out of my summery gray skirt and pocketed baby-chick-yellow tissue tee and into the dress. It zipped up the side easily. I turned to look in the full-length mirror.

The dress hugged my body in the right places and, at the same time, wasn't too revealing. The color made my fair skin look like it was carved from ivory rather than the cadaver pallor I sometimes had with the wrong shade of blue. My dark hair was stark against the silver blue of the dress. Even in its current disheveled state, it looked glamorous and shiny, and it even brought out the pale, pale blue of my eyes. I looked in the mirror even closer. My eyes matched my dress exactly. I only hoped Bri and Ana felt the same as I did about the dress.

Okay, here went nothing.

I stepped out of the dressing room where Ana and Brielle were waiting.

"Buy it!" Brielle shouted, seeming unable to control herself.

Ana nodded furiously. "Don't even try on another dress. It's perfect!" She'd never just say that to speed up our shopping—I knew she meant it. Aside from the fact that Ana didn't care much for dresses, and she obviously cared for this one, she also tended not to say anything unless she felt she had something valuable to contribute.

I didn't need any more convincing—this was *the* dress.

"Thanks, guys! I love it. I'm thinking a new pair of crystal drop earrings and a simple silver necklace from home—oh! The blue topaz pendant my mother bought me when I started at Yates."

Brielle was already nodding her head in agreement. "Tay is going to pass out when he sees you."

We all giggled until a salesclerk with pretty blond highlights and a stunning sapphire sundress came up to me. "Excuse me for interrupting, miss," she said finally.

"I was just about to change out of this," I cut in. "Don't worry, I'm buying it."

"No," she said, holding out a hand defensively. "I just wanted to tell you that dress is beautiful on you—it fits like a glove. I'm *glad* you're buying it. I was coming over to tell you that the dress sometimes finds its owner. A lot of people think it's the opposite—but, looking at you now—I'd say that dress has found its home."

I knew I was blushing, but I didn't even care. I felt like Cinderella finding her prince. Only, according to Brielle, *I* was the fairy godmother and instead of my prince, it was the dress I'd found. Or maybe the other way around.

Once I'd purchased the dress and a pair of sparkly crystal drop earrings that were *très chic* and lovely, I was ready to focus attention on Brielle.

I looked at the dresses that Ana and Brielle were carrying.

"You find anything to try on yet?" I asked.

"Three," she said. "But I need your opinion."

"Definitely," I said. "Go put one on and we'll wait out here."

Brielle took her three dresses into the room with her, and Ana and I sat on a cushy vintage settee with gold trimming and upholstery that looked like it was straight out of *The Great Gatsby*.

While we waited, my phone chimed and I grabbed it out of my purse.

It was a BBM.

Taylor:

What time should I pick you up?

Lauren:

7:30 ok?

Taylor:

Perfect. Can't wait 2 c u.

Lauren:

Thanks! Finishing up last min shopping with A and B then going home 2 get ready.

Taylor:

LOL. Good luck w B. I know how much she needs u 2 choose her whole wardrobe. Don't let her keep u.

Lauren:

☺ Not 2 worry—she'd never b late 2 a dance.

Taylor:

True. C u soon!

I put my phone back in my purse.

"How's Taylor?" Ana asked, playing with a tag on one of the dresses.

"Good," I said. "Glad school's over. Ready to party tonight."

"You never said, so I just assumed . . . he's okay about Canterwood, right?" Ana's voice had a concerned tone.

"He's really happy for me," I said. "He wants to talk tonight so we can figure out how to make things work while I'm away."

"Don't worry. If any couple can make long distance work, it's you and Taylor," Ana said.

I realized I'd been very quiet about my nervousness regarding Taylor. Too quiet. I really wanted—no, needed— to voice my fears to my friends.

"I'm scared," I confessed. "I want us to stay together, but what if he doesn't feel the same way? He's popular— and let's face it, he could date any girl in our grade. Why would he choose to stay with a girl who lives hours away if he could be with any other girl at Yates?"

"He cares about you, Laur. No way he would do that, unless it was what *you* wanted. If it is mutual, then that's different. But if you're up for it? I know he'll be." Ana reached over, struggling not to drop one of Brielle's dresses, and touched my hand in a comforting gesture.

I sighed, relieved to have that off my chest. "Thanks, Ana. That really helped. I'm not half as freaked now as I had been."

We both looked up, in alarm at first, when a squeal came from inside the dressing room.

Ana and I laughed when we realized what was going on.

"I think someone found a dress," I said, in a singsong voice.

Brielle opened the door and stepped out.

"Oooo!" Ana said.

"Brielle!" I said, standing. "That color is *killer* on you!"

Brielle twirled for us. She'd found a lilac bandage dress with spaghetti straps. It was so delicate and soft—very different from the bold colors Bri usually wore.

"You were right about the light purple—I love it," Brielle said, looking in the three-way mirror. "I think this is the one."

"That's a record," Ana said. "I think I have to buy *you* Pinkberry instead."

Brielle smiled. "Deal. Plus, I already have the perfect earrings at home, so I'm set."

"You get dressed," I said. "We'll meet you at the counter."

Ana got up and started hanging Brielle's other dresses on the discard rack.

Once Brielle was out, she paid for her dress and we all left the store, heading to grab Pinkberry. Brielle called her mom as we walked. It was fun to hear her describe every stitch of her dress to her mother. I thought about it for a minute. Aside from horses, nothing made me happier than fashion. I couldn't wait to look at the extracurriculars in the Canterwood course catalog. We were required to take at least two (not that I'd already memorized the welcome packet front-to-back or anything). It would be beyond hot if they offered a course in fashion or something!

Ana bought Brielle and me each a Pinkberry—Brielle because she'd taken such a short amount of time finding her dress, and me because I'd played a role in Brielle's quick find. *And,* I suspected, because she still felt guilty about the way she and Bri had treated me.

But, sitting outside, I made a decision about my friends.

Brielle and Ana had been, and were still, my besties. Sure, we all fought and made mistakes—huge, hurtful ones, even.

But we were linked together, always had been. We had fun together. We'd laughed and cried together and had *the* best shopping excursions ever.

It was official—the three of us were back. Besties for life.

18

JUST DANCE

BY THE TIME I GOT HOME, I WAS BACK IN THE red zone of stress. I only had an hour and a half to shower and do my hair (blow dry, curl, apply copious amounts of hair spray so as to be able to dance without losing my beachy waves, and finally shine spray), apply makeup, lotion, deodorant, get dressed, and finally, accessorize, slip into my silver flats, and re-gloss.

"Don't freak out," Becca said when I'd rushed by her room. "I'll help you."

Becca was going to her class's dance tonight, too, but hers started later than mine.

"Yes, please! And thanks!" I yelled on my way to my room. I hung my dress on my closet door and jumped into the shower.

I sat on my makeup chair, letting my hair air dry a little before blow drying. I pulled it back with a clip so it wouldn't be in the way while I applied makeup.

"How's it going, honey?" Mom asked, stepping into my room.

"I took the fastest shower ever and cut myself shaving in about six places, which are all invisible now, but it was worth it because I think I'm going to be ready on time," I said. "Oh, and Mom? Thanks for letting me buy that dress today."

"Of course," she said, eyeing it. "Wow, it is *gorgeous*. Tonight's a big deal." Mom added, smiling at me.

For once, she didn't seem halfway out the door. She acted like she really wanted to stay around and talk. "I'm really excited for you, Lauren. I know you're going to have fun with your friends. You worked hard this year, and I'm happy to see you get to have a fun night out with Taylor, Brielle, and Ana."

"Thanks, Mom." I tried not to let her see that I was nervous. And a little sad. And a little confused.

"Sweetie, you're probably feeling a lot of emotions right now," Mom said.

I should have known that Mom-radar would trump my pathetic acting skills.

"I guess I am," I said, focusing all my attention on the reflection in the mirror to apply concealer to a few red spots. "I mean, it's the last . . ." I couldn't finish.

Mom shook her head. "It may be the last Yates dance, but it's *not* the last time you're going to see your friends, Lauren. You've got amazing friends and a great boy-friend who all care about you deeply. Don't beat yourself up for wondering if you made the right decision about Canterwood."

I looked away from the mirror, meeting Mom's eyes with mine. I nodded.

"Just think about how you feel when you fall asleep at night," she added. "That's when you'll know—in your gut—if you're doing the right thing."

With one last my-daughter-is-growing-up-too-fast smile, she left me to finish my makeup.

I applied a hint of shimmery, rosy blush to my cheeks and applied a coat of clear, shiny lip gloss. Mom was right—tonight was about having fun and celebrating the end of sixth grade. Taylor and I were going to be fine. The last thing I wanted was to be sad at my final Yates dance.

I swiped brown-black mascara on my top eyelashes and smiled at myself, satisfied with my makeup. I let my hair out of the clip. It fell around my shoulders in clouds of dark, damp waves. I turned my hot pink Conair hair dryer on high and blasted my very long, thick (read: impossible) hair until it was dry. Next, I divided my hair into sections, each section clipped together with a mini claw.

I rolled each section around my curling iron, spritzing each with a few pumps of Bumble and bumble hairspray. When every section had been curled and my hair looked sufficiently like Shirley Temple (the curls would fall within minutes, turning to pretty, beachy waves) I applied a thin mist of Bumble and bumble shine spray as the final touch. I got up, flicked off the bathroom light, pulled on my dress, and ran my fingers through my long tresses.

"Whoa," Becca said, stepping into my room. "Nice dress. And good job on the makeup."

"Thanks." I smiled at my sister. "Shoes, earrings, and a clutch that'll match and I'm ready."

"Don't forget this," Becca said. She held out the Burberry perfume that she *never* let me wear.

"Really?" I asked.

"Just don't use too much," she said, winking.

I sprayed a little on my wrists. I loved the scent— it was feminine and musky without being too heavy or flowery. Becca sat on my bed, watching as I put in my new earrings and slipped my feet into my silver Marc Jacobs ballet flats.

"What purse goes with this dress?" I asked Becca.

"Already ahead of you," Becca said. She went into my closet and came out with a long, slender silver clutch.

"Perfect," I said. "Thanks!"

I reapplied my gloss and slipped that, my money, student ID, and cell inside the shimmery purse. I'd finished just in time—Taylor would be here any minute.

"Have fun," Becca said, heading for my door. "My turn to get ready."

"Thanks for helping me." I smiled. "See you later tonight."

I smoothed my dress over my hips and walked down the stairs where Mom and Dad were waiting.

"Oh, sweetie," said Dad, practically teary. "You look so grown-up and pretty."

"Daaad." I shook my head, but hugged him, careful not to wrinkle my dress.

"Your dad's right," Mom said. "You look gorgeous, Lauren."

A knock on the front door made me jump a little. I hoped Taylor thought I looked pretty, too.

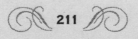

I walked to the door, smiling at his figure through the frosted glass.

"Hi," I said.

"Wow," he said, literally stepping back a tiny bit. "You look . . . beautiful isn't even good enough."

"Thank you." I couldn't stop the blush from spreading across my cheeks. "You look great, too."

Taylor had paired a black, long-sleeved button-down shirt with black-and-white pinstripe pants. He wore shiny black dress shoes, which I couldn't wait to see more of on the dance floor.

"Come in for a quick picture," Dad said.

I looked back. He was already holding up his camera. "*Super* quick," I said. "Or we'll be way later than fashionably late—which is *too* late."

I'd learned not to argue with Dad about pictures. He absolutely insisted, at every dance or big event, and I'd learned that it took more time for me to (unsuccessfully) talk him *out* of it than if I'd just gone along with it from the beginning.

Taylor and I stood in front of the stairs, and he curled his arm around my waist. I leaned into him, glad to have his arm around me. But I noticed something then—he seemed to pull away a little. I hid my frown. He was probably just nervous in front of my parents. We both smiled while Dad took his pictures.

"Time to go," I said. "Before you blind us both with that flash."

Dad waved us out the door and Taylor and I climbed into his mom's car. Mrs. Frost turned around, smiling at us.

"You look lovely, Lauren," she said. Mrs. Frost was so much nicer than Mr. Frost. She was way more relaxed. I was relieved that *she* was taking us tonight.

"Thank you," I said. "And thanks for picking me up."

"Exciting night, isn't it?" she said, pulling out of my driveway. "Sixth grade is over—are you glad?"

I sneaked a glance at Taylor. He stared out the window.

"Um, yes. I'm excited about summer," I answered.

Mrs. Frost smiled. I looked at Taylor again, unsure what was going on.

"Do you think they'll have sliders?" I asked him, bringing up his favorite party food.

"Maybe."

He didn't even look at me when he spoke.

"Everything okay?" I whispered.

That got his attention. Tay turned, locking eyes with me. He didn't look upset anymore.

"Sorry," he said, smiling. "I was just in my head." He

reached over, squeezing my arm. "I'm glad we're going."

"Me too. I thought you were mad at me for a minute."

He shook his head. "I'm not mad. Not at all."

Good—I'd misread him. Maybe he'd been sad that tonight was our last school dance together. Or maybe he was a little nervous, like I was, about talking later. I knew things were going to be fine, but talking about it was going to be hard. I could barely think about it without feeling sad myself.

We talked about silly, light stuff for the rest of the drive. Eventually, I saw the old Taylor, my boyfriend, smiling and laughing. It calmed me and the closer we got, the more excited I became about the dance.

My clutch vibrated. I opened it to see the red light on my BlackBerry blinking.

Ana:

I'm here! Where r u guys???

Lauren:

Pulling in driveway now.

Brielle:

2 mins away.

Ana was probably standing by the drinks table looking bored. She always did that until Brielle and I managed to convince her that dances were actually *fun*.

By the third or fourth song, she always got into it.

Before getting out of the car, Taylor and I thanked his mom and promised we'd meet her in the parking lot at ten. Taylor took my hand and, with dusk settling all around us, we walked up to the lit up school.

"Wow," I said as we got closer. Lights streamed out of every window from the huge gymnasium. Pop music blared from inside. The students were everywhere. Taylor reached into his pocket and handed our tickets to one of the chaperones—an English teacher I'd never had. Would never have.

"Enjoy," she said.

Taylor and I walked in through the side entrance. Navy and white, the school colors, were *everywhere*.

"Whoa," Taylor said, his tone echoing mine from just seconds earlier.

The entire gym had been transformed. The bleachers were folded up and gone. The wooden floors had been polished. Twirly streamers of all different lengths hung every few feet, and students had made GO YATES and YATES IS #1 banners on the walls.

"If only they'd had these decorations up when I'd been doing Coach Raymond's evil crunches," I said.

"I know," Taylor laughed. "It would have made running laps so much more fun."

We meandered around and found Ana standing exactly where I'd imagined—by the drink table.

"Are you guys hearing this?" Ana asked, tipping her head in the direction of the DJ.

"How could we *not*?" I asked.

Taylor filled a clear cup with bright red punch and handed it to me.

"Thank you," I said.

Tay and I smiled at each other and I stood on my tip-toes to kiss his cheek.

Whistles erupted behind us. I turned to find four of his friends from the swim team giving him the thumbs up.

Taylor waved a hand at them. "Be right back," he told me.

I moved closer to Ana who, I noticed upon closer inspection, had something sparkly on her eyes. I leaned just inches away from her face, inspecting her. Her routine—cat eyes only—was gone. She'd put an honest effort into tonight's dance. She'd swept her shoulder-length, light brown hair into a messy updo. Bobby pins with rhinestone hearts secured her Audrey Hepburn–like hair.

I'd been so taken in with the decorations, I hadn't paid

enough attention to Ana's makeup—not to mention her outfit.

"No way," I said. "Are you wearing more than just eyeliner? Ana!"

She blushed, bowing her head to sip her punch. "I *might* have decided to put in a little extra effort tonight. But! Don't think for even one second that I'm into this dance."

"No, of course not," I said, my tone teasing. "That hadn't even crossed my mind. But, Ana. You look seriously beautiful."

She had lined her top lids with a thin line of black eyeliner and brushed on a barely there coat of dark brown mascara (complete with curled lashes!) and had dusted her lids with a shimmery, sandy shade of eye shadow. Her lips, like mine, shone in the light, clear and glossy. There was even a hint of blush on her freckled cheeks.

"Thanks, Laur," Ana said, letting out a big breath. "I wanted tonight to be amazing. It's weird, but I actually felt like getting dressed up a little. You and Brielle always look so amazing at dances. I wanted to try it out for a change."

"Your makeup *and* clothes look amazing—they're very you, Ana."

I took in her outfit—she'd paired a black ruffled

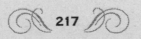

skirt with a satin ruby red capped-sleeve shirt with pearly buttons. She'd accessorized with skinny silver hoops and a pair of diamond studs in the second holes in her ears.

Ana smiled. "I'm comfortable in this—I wouldn't have felt that way in a dress like yours or Brielle's, though."

"That's the most important thing about fashion," I said. "Rule number one: If you wear clothes that you really love, ones that make you feel good about yourself and also make you feel comfortable, not only will you look great because of the clothes, but you'll feel confident. Nothing makes you look better than confidence, Ana. No matter how impressive the label or how glitzy the accessory. You look incredible tonight because you're glowing with confidence."

"I'm going to miss you, Lauren," Ana said.

We smiled at each other. Over my shoulder, I saw Taylor talking to his swim team buddies. I caught his eye and motioned that I'd be near the snacks whenever he was done.

"Be right there," he mouthed, holding up one finger.

I didn't care that he was hanging with his friends. It wasn't my style to be a clingy, stay-by-my-side-every-second girlfriend. I wanted to party with my friends, too. But I couldn't shake the way he'd been acting earlier.

"Let's grab something to eat and talk," I suggested.

Ana followed me, and we both grabbed plates that said YATES in bold navy letters on the bottom.

"There's so much food," Ana said. "I think Brielle was in charge of that."

"Is she here yet?" I asked, craning my neck to look around for her.

Ana scanned the room, then pointed. "There she is."

I followed Ana's gaze. Brielle was already on the dance floor. She'd always been an amazing dancer—she took ballet lessons on days off from riding. Will was dancing next to her and, from the look on his face, Bri had him totally hooked.

"They look great together!" I said.

Will, dressed in a button-down white shirt and black dress pants, held his own next to Brielle. His olive-toned skin, dark brown hair, and hazel eyes were all gorgeous.

I noticed that Bri had curled her dark hair into waves that cascaded around her shoulders, which she'd dusted with iridescent shimmer body powder. Brielle had paired her dress with white-silk kitten heels and a simple, layered silver necklace.

She looked away from Will, spotting me and Ana. She smiled and mouthed, *"Hi!"*

We waved to her.

"I'm so happy for her," Ana said. "She really, *really* wanted to go with Will. I bet they're the It-Couple next year."

"For sure," I said.

I reached for a serving spoon from the food table. I loved fruit and I'd just spotted marshmallow fruit salad that I wasn't passing up. I put a heaping spoonful on my plate, suddenly realizing that I'd had nothing but a slice of pizza and a small Pinkberry all day. Ana, a Mexican food addict, went in the opposite direction. She filled her plate with tortilla chips, a spicy jalapeño dip, and sour cream. I added a cupcake to my plate—vanilla with strawberry buttercream frosting.

We found two free chairs next to each other and sat down. I dug my fork into the fruit salad and gobbled three bites before Ana had even finished two chips.

Taylor spotted me and started to break away from his friends, motioning that he'd be right over.

"How's everything with you two?" Ana asked, her voice low and close to my ear so no one else would overhear.

"Um . . . it was a *little* weird on the ride here," I

admitted. "I think he's sad that I'm leaving. He's probably trying not to say anything about it because he doesn't want to hurt my feelings."

"You're sad to leave him, too," Ana pointed out, crunching down on a chip. "If Tay were *my* boyfriend, I'd be upset if he *wasn't* sad."

"Exactly. It's complicated—I mean, I certainly don't want him to be sad. But I do want him to at least tell me that he'll miss me. I know that's selfish."

"Not really," Ana said. "Of *course* you want your boyfriend to think about you. Especially after you just told him you'd be moving hours away for boarding school."

Ana and I saw that Taylor was getting closer to us.

"Just remember," said Ana. "You don't have to figure everything out tonight. It's not like it'll be the last time you see each other. You've got all summer to figure out Lauren-and-Taylor with Canterwood in the picture."

Ana had made me feel so much calmer. I wanted to pick her up and spin her around. "You're so right," I said, hearing the change of tone in my own voice. "I kept thinking, *Tonight's it! Everything has to be figured out before the dance is over.*"

Ana shook her head. "Not at all."

We smiled at Taylor once he reached us. He smiled back and sat next to me. Between hanging with his friends and sitting down with me and Ana, he'd filled his own plate with sliders, BBQ-flavored chips, and a couple of chocolate-chip cookies.

"Sorry about that," he said. "I didn't mean to ditch you as soon as we got here."

"You didn't *ditch* me," I said. "Ana and I were hanging out, too. Totally fine."

Taylor and Ana had always gotten along very well. The three of us fell into easy conversation about summer.

"You're going to have to fight us for time with Lauren this summer," Ana told Taylor in a joking tone. "Brielle and I are planning to steal her as often as we can."

Tay tilted his head. "You're *so* on." He looked at me. "You better get out your calendar and start filling it in. This is serious business."

"Poor me." I smiled at them. "Being wanted by my three best friends. This is terrible!"

Once we'd all finished eating, Taylor took all of our plates to the trash.

"Ana?"

Ana and I looked up at Jeremy, a gorgeous, highly sought after boy in our grade.

"Um . . . Jeremy?" Ana's voice was squeaky.

He smiled at her, flashing a set of perfect white teeth. "Do you . . . want to dance with me?"

Oh, snap! Ana's eyes darted to me. I wished I could high-five Ana right then and there. If this didn't prove my point about confidence being the most important rule of fashion, nothing would.

YES! SAY YES! I screamed at her in my head—trying to signal with my eyes to go with him. But Brielle and I had barely gotten Ana to agree to come to the dance. There was no way she'd say—

"Sure," Ana said. "I'd love to. Thanks!"

I couldn't stop my mouth from falling open. I looked like a total cliché, but I didn't care. I was absolutely stunned.

Ana tossed me a quick smile, smoothed her black skirt and got up, winking at me before she went off with Jeremy—who totes looked happy.

I half-stood, wanting desperately to get Brielle's attention. I signaled her with an exaggerated wave, looking like an idiot. But it worked.

"What?" she mouthed, her arms around Will.

"Ana!" I mouthed back, nodding in the direction of Ana and Jeremy who were dancing together. Dancing! And laughing.

Once Brielle saw what I was gesturing toward, her face mirrored my own clichéd one from earlier. She whispered something in Will's ear, then hurried over to me.

"How did *that* happen?" Brielle asked. "Ana's dancing. At a dance. With a guy. With . . ." She squinted Ana's way. "Oh. My. God."

"I know! He came over and I even felt sorry for him before he even said anything—I mean, I was *sure* Ana would say no. But before I could bribe her with a trip to the art store, she got up on her own and just went with him!"

"Wow." Brielle shook her head, still staring at Jeremy and Ana. "Our little Ana—all grown up."

We both pretend sniffled-slash-dabbed imaginary tears and giggled.

"I won't keep you, but are you having a crazy fun time with Will?" I asked.

The sparkle in Brielle's eyes was unmistakable. "He's so funny and cute. And smart. I wish we could stay all night. How about you? Where's Tay?"

"Ready to dance," I said. "And here comes Taylor."

Brielle winked at me. "Catch up with you later," she said before giddily running back to the dance floor.

Taylor started to sit back down next to me, but I stood, grabbing his hand. "Dance with me."

He smiled. "I thought you'd never ask," he joked.

We found an empty space on the packed floor, walking past a bunch of people I knew on our way. It still amazed me when no one said hi—I barely even got a half smile from a couple of girls I'd done a history project with about a month ago. Because of me, those airheads had all gotten A's. Rudeness, *ladies*?

But I kept my head up. I wasn't going to let *anyone* make me sad tonight, least of all *them*. Besides, the more I spoke to Becca, Ana, and Brielle about it, the more I realized that if people were actually going to behave this way, they weren't my real friends anyway.

Taylor and I moved to the rhythm of the music. He smiled at me whenever I looked at him, but something still felt off. I didn't know what was wrong. But I didn't want to keep bugging him about it either. Taylor would talk to me if there was something serious going on. I'd just have to trust him when he told me nothing was wrong.

When the fast music changed to a slow song, I stepped closer to Taylor, putting my arms around him. Smiling.

"I'm so glad we came," I told him. "I'm having a lot of fun."

"Good," Taylor said. "Me too."

We danced, shifting slowly back and forth. I knew he'd

wanted to talk about us tonight, but Ana's words from earlier were in my brain. I didn't have to settle everything or even *anything* tonight.

"Taylor, I know you wanted to talk about us tonight," I said. "And I want to talk, too, but do we really want to do that here—tonight?"

I shifted away from Taylor's ear so I could see the expression on his face. I could see the relief in his eyes.

"We have *all* summer together," I went on, encouraged. "Do you want to just . . . enjoy tonight and figure out us later?"

Taylor's eyes never left me "I thought about that too. This isn't the place. I just want it to be you and me when we get into all that. Tonight's supposed to be a party—we definitely deserve to enjoy it!"

I hugged him. "I'm so glad you agree."

Tension seeped from my neck and shoulders, my body loosening as we moved on the floor. The music picked back up and Taylor and I grinned at each other while we danced. I noticed that his posture had relaxed, too.

Tonight, sixth grade would get the send-off it deserved.

19

JUST ANOTHER
ORDINARY SATURDAY

THE NEXT MORNING, I WOKE UP WITH A SMILE
on my face.

My first thought was of the dance. Taylor and I had
danced until we'd exhausted ourselves. And before his
mom picked us up, we'd stepped into a quiet corner of
the room. First, we promised to BBM each other over the
weekend.

Then, Taylor had kissed me. Every time we kissed it
felt special.

I touched my lips with my index finger. They *still* felt
tingly—like I'd just woken up after a trip to the dentist
and the Novocain was beginning to wear off.

After our kiss, Taylor said good-bye to his friends and
I found Brielle and Ana. Brielle was sitting with Will, their

heads close together as they talked. I told her I'd text her tomorrow and gave her a hug before leaving. Ana was still on the opposite side of the floor with Jeremy.

"Hey," I'd said. "Sorry to interrupt, but I wanted to say bye before Taylor and I left."

"I hope you had fun," Ana said, hugging me. Then she leaned into me and whispered, "Jeremy's awesome."

I grinned.

"Did you have a good time?" I asked Jeremy.

I didn't know him that well, but we'd talked a couple of times.

"Really great," Jeremy said with a smitten look on his face. "I didn't know that Ana was an artist, too."

"I didn't know *you* were," I said. "That's cool! What's your specialty?"

"I mostly sketch and paint," he said.

"We've been talking about art all night," Ana said.

I'd never heard her like this. She sounded so happy and her voice was flirty.

"I'm glad you asked my best friend to dance," I told Jeremy. "See you guys later."

I left them, and before I was two feet away, they were already back to talking.

I snapped out of last night's memories and climbed out

of bed, not wanting to be late for my first riding lesson of the summer. Kim had changed weekend hours so that my lesson now started an hour later, but I wanted to get to the stable at my usual time. Every second I wasn't with my friends and family, I planned to spend at the stable.

Because in a few months, I'd be at Canterwood.

No matter how many shows I'd competed in or how many teams I'd ridden for, Canterwood was completely different. Canterwood wasn't like anything I'd experienced before. I knew I couldn't take Cricket with me and there was no way to predict what kind of school horse I'd get, so I had to prepare myself as much as I could. That meant riding. Lots and *lots* of riding.

I pulled on tan breeches and a ballet pink distressed tee before heading downstairs. Mom and Dad were at the breakfast table, sipping coffee and talking.

"Morning," I said, cheerful.

They both looked at me, smiles on their faces.

"What?" I asked slowly. "What's going on?"

"Come sit for a second," Dad said, patting the seat next to him with his palm. "Your mom and I want to talk to you."

Oh, no. Had Headmistress Drake changed her mind? Maybe Canterwood didn't want me anymore.

I almost saw spots as I sat down slowly. "Did Canterwood change its mind?" I said, unable to keep it in. "Are you trying to find a nice way to tell me? Because if you are, I'd rather just know now. Just . . . tell me."

"No, honey. No!" Mom said, putting her hand over mine. "You're still going to Canterwood—no one's going to change their minds. That's not it at all."

"Oh." I slumped in my chair, the spots beginning to dissipate one by one. I remembered how to breathe and put that action into practice.

Dad cleared his throat, looking from Mom to me. They were still making me nervous. I wished they'd just tell me what was going on.

"Lauren, your mom and I have been talking a lot about Canterwood," Dad said. "We're just so proud of you for getting accepted. We didn't give you a gift for your big acceptance—or for graduation—because we had to wait."

I shook my head, confused. "I didn't expect a gift, but wait, why did you have to wait?"

"We had to wait for Kim," Mom said.

The more either of them said, the more confused I got! "Kim? Why?"

"Honey, your mom and I wanted to give you something that you've deserved for a long, long time. You've always done well in school. But you've had *outstanding* grades at Yates. You're a responsible young woman. And when you got accepted into Canterwood . . . we asked Kim for help. To connect us with a few local breeders."

All I could do was just stare. And I still had no clue where they were going with any of this.

Mom laughed, touching my hand. "Lauren, next week, we're going to start looking for your very own horse. You deserve it. We'd really like you to have your own horse at Canterwood."

"Breathe," Dad said, grinning at me.

"Oh. I mean, *oh*. A horse. That's . . ." All I could do was giggle. I felt hysterical. "Are you . . . you're not *kidding*?"

"We're very serious," Dad said. "We talked to Kim about it and she also agreed that you needed a horse to train and grow with at Canterwood."

"A horse," I repeated in shock. "My own horse!"

"You've always ridden stable horses, which Kim thinks made you a stronger rider," Mom said. "But it's time. You're going to have your own horse, Lauren."

"I can't. Believe this," I whispered.

It felt like my brain was going to explode.

I hadn't even thought about a horse of my own. It just . . . never occurred to me. Canterwood had been enough all on its own—I'd been excited to just ride any horse they had. But now I was getting a horse that was *mine*—a horse I could name. And love. And never have to share with anyone if I didn't want.

My. Own. Horse.

"We had to wait because Kim had to call reputable farms in the area first," Mom explained. "She wanted to be there. To help you choose a horse that fits you best. Your dad and I don't know anything about horses, so we wanted to make sure we could work with her schedule next week. To visit the farms with us. *All* of us."

It was really starting to sink in now. My own horse! "This is the best present *ever*!" I said, my voice finally coming out above a whisper. I jumped up, hugging Mom and Dad. "Thank you! Thank you!"

"You're welcome, sweetie," Dad said. "Thank you for being the kind of daughter we trust enough to give a present like this. We can't wait to find the perfect horse for you, baby."

"I promise I'll be even more responsible," I said. "You won't have to worry about a thing. I'll—"

Mom shook her head, laughing now. "Laur, you don't have to tell us that. We aren't worried at all. You've treated every horse you've ever ridden as if it were your own.

You could have handed them off to a groom like a lot of the kids I've seen. But you never have. You've more than proven your responsibility."

"Thanks, Mom." Maybe Mom paid more attention to me than I'd thought. I turned to Dad, tears spilling down my cheeks now. "Dad," I said, my voice wobbly. "Thank you."

Dad smiled. "We start looking Monday morning, Laur-Bell. Just be prepared. Kim will want you to try a *few* horses. It'll be hard, so don't fall in love with the first horse you ride. And don't worry if it takes awhile to connect with the right horse. We've got plenty of time."

I nodded. "I know. I definitely want to find the absolute right horse. Oh my God, I have to tell Brielle and Ana. They're going to *freak*! Dad, can we go?"

"Go get your boots, Bell. We'll go right away."

I jumped up, hugging them each again before dashing to my closet to grab my boots. I shoved my feet into them, then realized I needed my bag. Then I realized something bigger than my bag. Becca! I yanked my boots off (house rules) and ran to Becca's bedroom. The door was closed. I knew she was still sleeping, but I *had* to tell her *now*. Otherwise, I'd burst.

"Becs?" I said softly, opening her door.

She shifted, opening one eye and looking at her clock all frowny. "Lauren. It's the first day of summer vacation. That means sleeping in!"

"Sorry! I know. Sorry. I have to tell you something really quick, then I'll let you go back to sleep—I swear." I sat beside her on her bed, controlling my instinct to duck.

Becca rose up on her elbows, her long hair in a messy ponytail. "This better be good," she grumbled.

"Mom and Dad just told me about my graduation present," I said. "I'm getting a horse!"

Becca smiled, sitting up all the way. "You have no idea how hard it was to keep *that* a secret."

"You knew?!"

"For a few weeks," Becca said, awake now. "They told me on the condition that I'd promise not to tell. I'm really happy for you, Bell. You need your own horse."

"I can't believe I'm actually getting one," I said. "I'm *freaking out!*"

Becca laughed. "Really? Hard to tell. Now go to your lesson and tell Bri and Ana."

Another wave of excitement washed over me. "See you later!"

I started to get off Becca's bed, but she grabbed my

arm. At first, I was scared this might turn into another shoe-throwing incident.

But instead, she hugged me. "Congratulations, Laur."

I hugged her back.

Hard.

"Thanks, Becs."

My eyes filled again. Okay, this needed to stop! *Go away*, I commanded my tears. They didn't, or at least not until Becca let me go.

"Now go. And never wake me up this early ever again." But Becca smiled as she said it.

"Deal," I said, laughing.

I closed her door behind me and grabbed my phone, bag, and boots. I ran back down the stairs. I was buckled and ready in the car before Dad was even out the front door.

I took out my phone. I wasn't going to tell Taylor, Brielle, *or* Ana over BBM. This was too big. But I could at least tease Brielle and Ana with my news the way Bri had teased Ana and me about Will.

Lauren:

I have *big* news. Like, epic!!!!

My fingers fumbled over the tiny buttons—I was shaking so bad I could barely type.

Brielle:

EPIC news?!

Ana:

What???? TELL us. Now!!!

Lauren:

I want 2 wait till I c u guys! This is major, in-person news. I'll be @ BC soon.

Brielle:

pouts Fine. Make us wait, then!!

Ana:

U better spill the sec u c us!

Lauren:

I will! Swear! U won't believe it!

Brielle:

☺

Ana:

Let me guess: you got into the most elite equestrian boarding school in the entire country. Nope, that was weeks ago. Old news. JK! What B said.

Lauren:

Hahaha—B, did you know A became a standup comedienne? JK back! C u guys v v v soon!

When Dad got in the driver's seat, I put my phone down. I'd call Taylor after my lesson and tell him. I was too excited to be on the phone right now—not after the news Mom and Dad had just given me!

"Has it sunk in yet?" Dad asked, starting the engine.

"I keep going back and forth," I said. "One minute, I can't believe it's really going to happen. Then the next, I'm already picturing trying out all the different horses."

Dad pulled down the visor, shielding his eyes from the morning sun. "Your mom and I knew from the day you got accepted that we wanted to get you a horse. We just had to make sure that Kim was available to help. And we didn't want to just overwhelm you with everything all at once."

"Canterwood was a big shock," I said. "I might have had a heart attack if you'd told me that I was getting a horse the next day."

Dad chuckled. "Okay," he said after a pause. "Tell me, what are some things that are important to you in a horse?"

I thought for a minute. No one had asked me that question before.

"Well, I don't care one bit whether it's a mare or a gelding. But I really don't want a horse that's too green because I'd have to train it—and I'm still learning myself. At the same time, I don't want a horse that's *too* well trained.

There's no challenge in that. I'd love to have a horse that's ready to show *and* that's ready for the heavy workload that I know goes along with riding for Canterwood."

Dad nodded. "All of that sounds very smart. And what about *you*, Bell? Is there anything your mom or I can do this summer to make things easier for you? Whatever it is—I want you to tell us."

Anything else? Like buying me a horse and moving to Connecticut so I could ride at Briar Creek where the head instructor had a connection to my dream school, which was an expensive boarding school I'd subsequently gotten into while they supported me the whole way—like all that wasn't enough? Yeah, they really need to step it up. But nonetheless, I considered Dad's offer.

"There is *one* thing I'd be in to if anyone has time," I said. "Can we go visit Canterwood before I move in? I think seeing it in person might make me less nervous."

"Of course," Dad said. "I think that's a *great* idea, Laur-Bell. I'll check my calendar as soon as I we get home."

"That's all then," I said. "I mean, aside from getting some dorm stuff, doing summer assignments, pre-class reading, and riding . . ."

Dad flipped on his blinker, changing lanes. "Getting stuff for your new room will be fun! And it's not *ideal* doing classwork over the summer, but you'd have had to do that for Yates anyway. And you love riding, so I can't see that becoming one of those things you dread doing. You'll get it done, Bell—you've got all summer. Knowing you, it'll be done before the end of the week."

Dad had a way of not only making things seem less daunting, but making them even seem exciting. He also loved to kid me about my self-discipline. He'd never done well with school and was a huge, self-proclaimed procrastinator. So it amused him to no end that he'd raised a daughter who not only dreamed of being vale-dictorian someday, but who was also known to finish homework on Friday nights. Hey, it makes the weekends more fun when all of the book stuff isn't hanging over your head every day.

I took a breath. "You're right," I said. "I'll just make a list and check things off as I go."

"That's my girl. Make sure you put 'buy extra list-making paper' on your shopping list for school," Dad said. It was his most favorite joke. I had to smile.

"I *did* just get a new Pottery Barn Teen catalog the other day," I said. "It had really cool dorm stuff. Like a whiteboard that is also half corkboard. It would be perfect for hanging up important papers and due dates. And"—I threw this one in just for him—"I could use a whiteboard to make a giant to-do list."

Dad and I smiled at each other. I was the first one to break into a fit of giggles. But he was a close runner-up, laughing all the way to Briar Creek.

"See?" Dad said. "You and your mom can spend a whole day shopping for your room. What girl wouldn't want two rooms to decorate and fill with a bunch of cool stuff?"

We pulled into Briar Creek's driveway and Dad pulled up to the stable.

"Cool stuff, Dad?"

He nodded.

"Tell you what," I said. "I'd love for you make *me* a list of your ideas of cool stuff. No help from Mom!"

"Yes!" he said, giving me a thumbs up. What a dork!

"First thing on my list: a turntable."

I covered my face with my hands.

"Oh, man, I love a good challenge—especially in list form," he said, making himself (and me, I admit it) laugh.

"Second cool stuff idea: lava lamp," he said.

I considered the suggestion.

"Actually," I told him, "those are coming back."

"No!" he said.

"Yes," I countered back. "I'm telling you—they were *in* the PB Teen Catalog."

"No," Dad said, a look on his face that seemed to communicate that he was proud of his knowledge of trends.

"I *even*," I continued, deciding to give him one last morsel of happiness, "saw a light blue one with glitter floating around in it."

Dad stared at me for a minute. "You *like* this lava lamp," he deduced. "You want it in your room. It's your favorite color, and it comes with glitter, which you love. I'll tell you what, Bell. That lava lamp is *yours*. Consider it done."

We laughed until I was crying and Dad was rubbing his eyes.

When I looked up, I spotted Brielle's mom backing out of her parking spot. Right by where the car had been, Brielle walked over to Ana. They looked over, saw me, and waved.

"Have a good lesson and I'll pick you up later," Dad said. "I'm serious about that lamp—it's going with you to Canterwood."

I grabbed my bag and got out of the car. My hand rested on the open passenger door. I leaned in and blew my dad a kiss, thanked him *again*, and then said, "About that lamp? I'm counting on you now. That lamp is coming with me."

Dad smiled. "Count on it, Bell. I love you."

"I love you, Dad," I said. I was the luckiest person in the world to have my parents. Yeah, they were embarrassing sometimes, but more than anything, they loved me. And they supported my dreams in every way possible.

I grabbed my bag and got out of the car.

"Get over here!" Ana shouted, bouncing. "What's going on?"

Brielle cocked her hip. "Hello?! You're *killing* us." She put her helmet in her other arm.

"I know, I'm sorry. It was so huge," I said. "I couldn't tell you guys over BBM."

"Lauren!" Ana and Brielle shouted at the same time.

"I'm getting a horse!" I blurted.

"Omigod," Brielle squealed.

"Omigod!" Ana shrieked.

They grabbed me in a huge hug.

"I know! Mom and Dad told me right before today's lesson. I thought they were kidding."

"That would be a pretty mean joke," Ana said.

"I know," I said. "But I'd just woken up! It seemed like a dream. I never expected a *horse*. They told me it was my graduation present and that they wanted me to have a horse for Canterwood."

"You deserve your own horse," Ana said. "You've been riding forever and you've never had one."

"It's perfect timing," Brielle said. "What kind of breed do you want? When are you going to look?"

I loved that my friends were as excited as I was. A lot of people would have been too jealous to even ask one question, but my besties, riders themselves, really got it.

"I haven't even thought about the breed," I admitted. "Something a little bigger than Cricket. Dad said that we're going to the first breeder on Monday. It's going to be the longest weekend of my life probably," I groaned.

"I know! I'd die waiting, too," Ana said. "But we'll keep you busy. Did you tell Taylor yet?"

We started toward the stable.

"I'll call him later," I said. "There wasn't any time before practice. And I don't want to tell *him* over BBM either."

"He'll be so excited for you," Brielle said. She pulled her enviable silky black hair back and gathered it into a messy bun.

"I can't wait to tell him." I blinked through the darkness as my eyes adjusted to the shaded stable. "There are tons of things to look forward to. I might explode. At least today will be packed with riding. And Sunday, I'll probably start putting together some ideas for my new room. I need to figure out what I have to take—I think there's a page on Canterwood's Web site with that info."

"Lauren, you're beyond lucky," Brielle said. "I wish I could talk my mom into redoing my room. It hasn't changed since I was, like, ten. I love pink, you know I do, but I don't want pink *walls* anymore."

Brielle had been pleading with her parents for months for a room makeover. I'd been there thousands of times, and I had to admit, it was pretty frilly even for her. I had a feeling it would have been too stereotypical "little girl!" for Malibu Barbie, too.

Then I had an idea—one that would serve three purposes: It would help Bri to think of her own ideas for a new room, it would make the time move along faster with me having my friends around, and it would also help me to create the best dorm room ever.

"This summer you guys have to help me pick out stuff for my dorm," I said. My besties had to put together the best room ever in the history of Canterwood.

"Oooh, definitely!" Ana said, her smile growing with every word. "I can start thinking of a good color scheme for you."

I stopped when we approached Kim's office. "I want

to talk to Kim for a sec, guys, but I'll meet you in the outdoor arena to warm up."

"See you there," Bri said, wiggling her fingers at me as she and Ana headed off to groom and tack up Zane and Breeze.

Kim's door was open. She turned around when she heard my footsteps.

"Well, hello there my little soon-to-be horse owner!" Kim said.

I leaned against the doorway, hoping it would hold me up in case my knees came out from under me from sheer excitement. "Kim, I can't believe all of this. Thank you so, so much for helping me and my parents. I know we're going to find the right horse with your guidance."

Kim rocked back in her desk chair. "You definitely will. It could take some time—or you could find the right horse immediately. Either way, try not to worry—you'll be going to Canterwood with a great horse."

I opened my mouth to say something, but hesitated. I didn't want Kim to think I was comparing myself to . . . *her* at all. I knew that she was way out of my league. But I wanted desperately to know. After all, her horse was nearly as famous at BC as she was. I tried again. "Like Sasha and Charm?"

"Like Sasha and Charm," Kim said.

As usual, Kim looked proud as could be at the mention of Sasha's name. But the way she looked at me now, I saw something new. Something I'd never seen before.

I must have looked as confused as I felt. Because, just as I was about to end my own guessing game, Kim confirmed a thought I didn't even dare think, let alone say out loud.

"Lauren Towers," Kim said, smiling. "I am so proud to have had the privilege to teach you."

I stood in the door, so struck by what Kim had said, it felt as though my feet were cemented to the ground. I wanted to thank her, to throw my arms around her and cry out with joy. But instead, I only watched as she got up from her desk, clapped me on the arm, and laughed warmly.

"Don't be late to practice, Towers," she said in a mock-tough manner.

When she left, I allowed myself thirty seconds of pure bliss. Without coming right out and saying it, Kim had said something that meant more to me than she'd ever know. Something so powerful, I knew I'd never repeat it aloud.

Kim had once looked at Sasha Silver the same way

she'd just looked at me. She'd looked at her and, at some point—I knew this as well as I knew any other certain thing in my life—she'd said the same thing.

"Sasha Silver," she'd once said. "I am so proud to have had the privilege to teach you."

Like Sasha Silver before me, I was moving on from Briar Creek to Canterwood Crest.

And Kim was proud of us both.

20

STAYING BUSY
ISN'T EASY

I BARELY SLEPT ON SATURDAY NIGHT.

I woke up early Sunday morning, grateful that it was finally a decent time of morning. I made a cup of blueberry green tea, and grabbed a notebook and a few catalogs to start making a list of what I needed for school.

Mom, the only one crazy enough to be up, walked over to where I was sprawled out on the comfy living room chaise longue.

"Trying to keep busy?" she asked, smiling.

"Trying is definitely the key word in that question. But *this* is fun. Look." I pointed to a poster. It was a black silhouette of a girl holding her horse's reins. The background was a bright, SweeTart pink. "How do you feel about this for my dorm room?"

"I love it," Mom said. "It's very *you*. Remember, Lauren, Charlotte's coming home in just a few days. She'll be able to give you lots of help since she lives in a dorm room."

In all of the craziness, I'd forgotten that my older sister would be home next week. She'd been finished with college for about a month and had been visiting friends before coming home. We weren't close the way Becca and I were, but it wasn't because we hated each other—we were just too far apart in age to really relate well to each other.

"Yeeeah," I said. But maybe I was wrong. Maybe she'd *want* to help me with this.

Mom smiled at me for a minute. But she didn't say anything. She turned, sidestepping the coffee table, and headed toward her office.

I picked up my phone and opened BBM. I still hadn't told Taylor my exciting news yet. We'd chatted over BBM briefly, but he'd said he couldn't talk. Maybe he'd be able to now—I was sure he'd be up—he always got up early like me.

Lauren:

U awake?

I went back to my catalog, looking at clothing storage options. Storage bins seemed like the most practical option. They were largest. I knew I couldn't stuff all my clothing into what would probably be a smaller closet, one-eighth the size of the one I had at home.

Cute.

I put one of my color-coded sticky tabs on a page featuring coffee-colored canvas bins adorned by polka dots. Each one had lids, which made them stackable.

I checked my phone again—no messages from Tay. *He must still be asleep,* I told myself.

I turned back to the catalog, scanning for accessory storage.

Canterwood had sent a follow-up e-mail yesterday that said I'd be given my roommate's contact info later on in the summer and we'd be able to 'meet' via e-mail. I wondered what my roommate would be like and if her style would be like mine or if she'd be totally different. Having a roommate I'd never met before was exciting and scary all at the same time!

Almost an hour later, my phone buzzed.

Taylor:

Awake now, lol. What's up?

Lauren:

Can u talk now? I rlly, RLLY have smthing 2 tell u!

Taylor:

Yeah, call me. I want 2 hear ur news.

I picked up my catalogs, notebook, and pen and went outside to the pool deck. There was a slight coolness to the early-morning May air. I put down my stuff on a table and dialed Taylor. Unable to sit—the news too exciting!—I paced barefoot on the deck.

"Hey," Taylor said, answering after what felt like ninety-seven rings.

"I've been going crazy waiting to talk to you," I said, cheerful.

"Sorry." Taylor yawned. "I was with the guys yesterday and they stayed over playing video games until really late. I didn't want to call *too* late and get you in trouble."

"Oh."

It stung a little that he couldn't have left his friends for a minute or two to return my call. But he was talking to me now. What was the point in being mad now? I was too excited!

"So, what's the big news?" Taylor asked, still sounding pretty sleepy.

"It's *really* big," I teased. "Yesterday, my parents told me they were giving me a present for graduation and for getting into Canterwood."

"So . . . what'd they give you?"

"They haven't given it to me yet. It's something I have

to pick out. They're giving me a horse!" My voice rose several octaves every time I said that.

"Lauren! That's great. You'll be completely ready for your new school now. I know how much you've always wanted a horse."

"Isn't it the best gift ever?" I was squeaking so loud, I scared a squirrel. It darted through the grass and up a tree, stopping to chatter at me, as though it was scolding me.

"That's really awesome—like getting your first car. I'm really happy for you."

"Thanks, Tay. I'm starting to look tomorrow—and I'm going insane attempting to stay busy."

Taylor laughed. "I bet."

We talked for a few more minutes before agreeing to BBM later so we could figure out a day next week to go out.

And I spent the rest of the day prepping for Canterwood in every possible way. By the time I went to bed, I had so many lists, they covered my bulletin board completely.

I fell asleep wondering what my new horse would be like.

21

ZERO CHEMISTRY

"IS THIS IT?" I ASKED FOR THE HUNDREDTH time.

"Yep," Dad said, looking at his GPS. "We're here." He made a right turn and we drove a short distance down a country road before I saw the fences.

Horses dotted the pasture. We turned down a driveway under a silver sign that said WILDEN FARM.

Mom had work this morning, so Dad had driven me to the stable. I'd Chatted with Brielle and Ana on the drive over, writing *@BrielleisaBeauty & @AnaArtiste Wish me luck!!* 9:02 a.m.

A new Chat symbol appeared on my phone just before we'd reached the stable.

*@LaurBell *tons of 4 leaf clovers* 9:24 a.m.*

I smiled at Brielle's message. Ana was at a weekend art class, so I doubted she had her phone on. I put mine away, looking up.

"There's Kim's truck," I said, pointing.

Dad pulled the SUV next to Kim's red truck and we got out. I'd dressed in breeches, a T-shirt, and paddock boots. I tucked my helmet under my arm, walking next to Dad as we headed for the stable's entrance.

"Hi," I said, spotting Kim inside.

"Hi, Lauren," Kim said. "Hi, Gregg," she said, shaking my dad's hand. "This is Jeffrey. He owns Wilden Farm, and he's got a couple of horses for Lauren to try out."

"Hello," I said, offering him my hand to shake.

Jeffrey, looking surprised, shook my hand and Dad's. He was an older man, probably in his fifties, and he had a kind smile.

"Polite young lady you've got there," he told Dad, nodding at me.

"We try," Dad said, laughing.

"Kim told me about your experience," Jeffrey told me. "I kept that in mind when choosing horses for you to ride. They've already been checked by a vet, I've got the paperwork to show you, and Kim's given them both a careful look."

"Wonderful," Dad said. "It's important that I find the exact right horse for my daughter."

Jeffrey nodded his understanding. "Come this way," he said, gesturing with a callused hand.

We all followed him to a large indoor arena. Inside, a groom held two horses that were already tacked up. My eyes didn't know where to look first! One horse was a chestnut mare with a stripe. The other was a blue roan gelding. Both were taller than Cricket, and my practiced eye took in their near-perfect conformation. They stood perfectly still, both flicking an ear forward as we approached.

"What are their names?" I asked, smiling at the well-behaved horses.

"The chestnut is Baylee and the gelding is Walker," Jeffrey said. "They're both four, so they're a *little* green, but I don't think you'll have any trouble with your experience."

"Have they competed?" I asked, unafraid to be as direct as possible. "I'm looking for a horse to show—my specialty is dressage."

"They've both shown," Jeffrey said. "Baylee has done more dressage work than Walker. Perhaps you'd like to try her first?"

"Okay." I put on my helmet and walked up to Baylee.

I patted her neck while the groom offered me her reins. "Thank you," I told him, gathering them in my left hand. I put my toe in the stirrup iron and swung into the saddle, settling lightly on Baylee's back. She stepped forward as if I'd signaled for her to go before I'd even gotten my other foot in the stirrup.

"Whoa," I said, my voice firm.

I gave the reins a short tug, halting her.

Bayleee snorted and put her ears back, but listened. I kept my body relaxed in the saddle, mentally preparing myself for anything she might throw at me. Baylee was either having an off day, acting out simply because I was new to her, or she was a little greener than I'd thought.

The mare and I made several laps around the arena. I strained to hold her at a trot and not let her break into a canter. Her mouth lathered with foam in just a few short minutes and her neck bowed under the reins. My arms shook from holding her back.

This wasn't working. Disappointment coursed through me even though I'd known better than to expect to fall in love with the first horse I rode.

I eased her to a walk and turned her back toward Jeffrey, the groom, Kim, and Dad.

"I'm very sorry," I said. "I don't want to put her through this anymore. We're just not clicking."

"No need to apologize," Jeffrey said, taking her reins so that I could dismount. "Not every horse and rider mesh. You'll find one—whether it's at my farm or from someone else."

Jeffrey was a good guy. Since Kim recommended him, I knew he would be. Another horse dealer could have tried to talk me and Dad into buying the first horse I rode—regardless of whether or not we were a match—just to sell the horse. But Jeffrey seemed to really care about making the right match between horse and rider.

"You gave it a shot," said Kim. "Lauren, why don't you give Walker a try?"

I mounted the roan. Walker was the opposite of Baylee. I had to ask him several times for a trot. For being four years old, he seemed to behave like a much older school horse who'd already been jaded by arena work.

Walker listened to every cue, moving through serpentines, a working trot, changing leads, and cantering around the arena.

But that was the problem. He actually felt too willing. There was no *fire* coming from him.

I eased him over to the group, patting his neck.

"He's so sweet," I said honestly. "I think he'd be perfect for a less experienced rider—he behaves quite mature for this age."

Kim turned to Jeffrey. "Lauren needs a horse who's a bit more of a challenge."

Jeffrey rubbed his bristly beard. "Okay," he said. "That's very helpful. I feel as though I know more about what you're looking for now, Lauren. I've got a few more I'd like you to consider. Would you be willing to come back later in the week and try them?"

I nodded, grateful.

"I'm sorry you had to get Baylee and Walker all ready," I apologized to the groom. Bryan, I'd heard Jeffrey call him.

Bryan smiled, shaking his red head. "It's my job. I'm Bryan, by the way. It was nice meeting you, Lauren. Good luck with your search."

"Nice to meet you," I said. "I'll probably see you later in the week. How long have you worked with Jeffrey?"

"I've worked here after school for a while now—I'm saving up for my first horse," Bryan said. "So I understand completely how important it is to find the right one."

I liked Bryan. The adults were deep in conversation

about the next step. I was glad to have someone closer to my age to talk to.

"It's harder than I thought it would be," I confessed, rubbing Baylee's neck. Now that I wasn't on her back, the mare was very quiet. "I feel bad saying no to any horse—I want all of them to go to a good home where they'll be treated well and be loved. But at the same time, I have to find a horse that works for me."

"Absolutely, and don't ever worry about Jeffrey's horses. He always makes sure they're paired with the right owner. Unless you'd come back a couple more times and had amazing rides with Baylee or Walker, he wouldn't have sold them to you."

"That makes me feel a *lot* better," I said. "Thanks."

"Lauren?" Dad walked over to me and Bryan. "Let's head out so Jeffrey and Kim can get back to their days. We'll come back later in the week so you can try a few more horses. Okay?"

"Sounds great," I said.

I thanked Jeffrey and Bryan again, then waved good-bye to Kim.

Once Dad and I got in the SUV, I let out a quiet sigh. I knew I should just be feeling grateful to have such an amazing opportunity. Still, I'd been waiting for this day with crazy anticipation. I couldn't help but feel a little down.

"Sorry I kept you away from work this morning," I told Dad. "I tried but neither of them felt right."

"Oh, honey, don't apologize. Kim told me this was going to take time—and I never want you to settle. You'll know when you find the right one. And we will."

"Thanks, Dad." I smiled at him. "So, what day are we coming back?"

"On Thursday," he said. "It was the next time Jeffrey and Kim were both free at the same time. But in the meantime, Kim mentioned she had a horse at another farm that she wanted you to try tomorrow."

I grinned, relieved that we had another horse to go see so soon. Thursday felt like such a long ways away.

I'd ride horses all summer long and wouldn't stop until I found *my* horse. I knew the one for me was out there—I just had to keep trying each one until I found the exact match.

I looked at Dad. I was so lucky that he was willing to drive me around trying all the horses I could. Not to mention Kim was there making sure everything went well no matter what farm we went to.

I was excited about tomorrow, but something in my

gut told me that it would be one of *Jeffrey's* horses that would eventually work out for me. He'd listened closely and watched to see to what I'd wanted. Now that he'd seen me ride, I felt sure he'd be able to use that to find my match.

When I got home, I BBM'd Brielle and Ana. There were already messages from them, waiting to hear how it had gone.

Lauren:

I tried 2 horses—a green mare and a trail horse. The 1ˢᵗ was 2 much and the other wasn't enough.

Ana wrote back a few minutes later.

Ana:

Sorry ☹ But at least u r out there looking.

Brielle:

Xactly. & u don't want 2 settle.

Lauren:

Def not! I'm going out 2mrw 2 another farm & back 2 Wilden on Thurs.

Brielle:

Kim will find u the perf Canterwood horse. Try not 2 feel down abt today.

Lauren:

Did @ 1ˢᵗ, but I had 2 be real—I knew I wouldn't find *the* horse on my 1ˢᵗ day looking.

Ana:

It's going 2 b that much better that u tried so many horses when u find the ONE.

Lauren:

☺ ☺ Thanks, A. I rlly think I'll find the right horse @ Wilden eventually. But I'm still giving 2mrws horse a shot, obvi.

Brielle:

Good! And I totally agree w Ana . . . ooo! Want us 2 come w/u on Thurs?

Lauren:

OMG, I'd love that. U guys would be so much help!

Ana:

I'm totally free—I'll be there!

Lauren:

Yay! Thx guys. TTYL.

Once we said good-bye, I sat still and listened to the commotion around me. Charlotte flew in on Wednesday, so Mom had Ellen here today to clean. Mom had even taken the day off work, which made her nervous since her BlackBerry was usually superglued to her hand. She was readying Charlotte's old room one door down from mine.

Ellen had been asked to stay overtime to clean the

house from top to bottom, which she graciously agreed to do. Mom wanted to make everything *perfect* for Charlotte's first day home.

Thinking about spending the summer with my older sister in the house made me a little nervous. I'd gotten used to it being just Mom, Dad, Becca, and me. Charlotte came home for holidays, but they'd always been short and there hadn't been time enough to find a reason for us to fight. Last year, though, Charlotte and I'd had a big blowout.

Just thinking about it didn't make me feel especially eager for her to come home. I imagined that she probably felt the same way about me.

I remembered it vividly. Charlotte had been packing to go back to school after coming home for spring break and had been hanging out with her old friends from high school.

"Dad said to tell you that he's taking me to my riding lesson and he'll be right back," I'd told her dutifully.

Charlotte sighed. She turned and tugged her long, straight blond hair out from its messy ponytail. She was gorgeous—the only blonde in our family, with pool blue eyes to match.

People always assumed that she was the pretty girl with

tons of boyfriends (which she was) but they also assumed pretty was all there was to her. They were wrong. Charlotte had graduated with highest honors and had gotten early acceptance to Sarah Lawrence. For every hour I put into riding, she put that much time into studying.

"Of *course* Dad's taking you to a lesson," she said, adding, "right before I leave," just under her breath.

"What does *that* mean?" I asked, stunned. "I can't drive *myself*."

She tossed a sweater into her suitcase. "Whatever, Lauren. I'm over it. I'm just glad I don't live here anymore."

It felt like she'd slapped me.

"Why?" I asked. "What did I do to you?"

"Please," she spat, facing me. "I'm so sick of everything being about *you*, Lauren. Did you ever think about how it was for me and Becca when either Mom or Dad—or both—were a thousand miles away at your fiftieth horse show? Or how it felt when they missed all *my* school stuff because they were out supporting *your* little hobby?"

"It's not a hobby!" I screeched defensively. "I'm a professional rider, Charlotte. You *know* that. You're so immature. Becca is way younger, but she actually gets it. She understands how important this is to me. You're my sister—I thought you understood, too."

Charlotte folded her arms. Her cheeks were cherry red. "You're not even going to apologize?"

"For what?" I asked. I honestly didn't understand why she'd gotten angry so quickly.

Charlotte laughed. "Forget it. Forget everything. What a little *brat*. I can't wait to get back to school, start classes again, and forget you and your idiotic horses even exist."

Do NOT cry! I told myself. I held back my tears and glared at my sister. I was always jealous of how gorgeous and smart she was. I worked three times harder than any of my classmates, just so I could be as smart as Charlotte one day. "I can't wait until you're gone," I said. "If you can't support me like a real sister would, then why are you even speaking to me?!"

For the first time, she looked ugly to me. So ugly, I couldn't bear looking at her old piggish face for another second. Suddenly, I whirled around and slammed her door so hard, it rattled the doorknob.

Mom and Dad had come upstairs when they heard the door, but I was in my room, refusing to speak at all, let alone about what my own sister had said to me. Charlotte wouldn't talk about it either. Becca came into my room. Eventually she rubbed my back while I cried into my pillow. I'd never wanted to take anything away from Charlotte and I certainly never meant to hurt her. But she'd never spoken to me about any of it before that day. I didn't realize I'd done anything to hurt anyone. Had I really been as selfish as Charlotte claimed? I felt sick, her words going around on a loop in my head.

I never loved Becca more than in that moment when she continued rubbing my back and reassuring me that she didn't agree with Charlotte at all, once I was finally able to get out what had happened.

I didn't want to think about Charlotte anymore. It made me too stomachache-y and anxious. Instead, I picked up my phone to BBM Taylor. He'd asked me to let him know how horse shopping had gone.

Lauren:

So I just got back from trying 2 horses!

He wrote back immediately.

Taylor:

How was it??

Lauren:

Not so great. They were good horses, but not the right fit for me.

Taylor:

Aw, sorry, Laur. But u r going to try more, right?

Lauren:

Yep! 2mrw and Thurs.

Taylor:

R u upset that u didn't find 1 2day?

Lauren:

I was @ 1ˢᵗ, but I knew they weren't right ones for me. I'll find the one—I've got all summer to look.

Taylor:

Def ☺

Lauren:

Got any plans on Fri? Haven't seen u 4 a while. Miss you.

Taylor:

Miss u 2, L. No plans. Want 2 go out?

Lauren:

Luv 2. Let's both think abt options and then talk abt them ltr.

Taylor:

Perf. And msg me abt the horses 2mrw.

Lauren:

I will. TTYS. ☺

Taylor:

☺

I put away my phone and pulled up Canterwood's Web site for the umpteenth time since I'd gotten my acceptance letter. I looked through the photo gallery of dorms, classrooms and—I stopped on the stable page.

That's where *my* horse was going to live.

I untacked a STUFF FOR HORSE <3 list from my board. Mom had said to go to State Line Tack online and put everything I needed in a cart. Later, she, Dad, and I would go through it together and see what I'd added before placing the order.

Shopping for horse stuff made it feel real.

Soon I'd be lacing a brand new halter onto *my* horse!

22

WHAT IF . . .

MOM, DAD, BECCA AND I PILED INTO THE
Range Rover on Wednesday afternoon. It was a trip I'd
been dreading.

We were on our way to pick Charlotte up from the airport. I tried everything I could think of not to go, including an attempt at faking sick that had ended very poorly
with me sticking the thermometer against a lightbulb that
had been on in my room for hours. Needless to say, I
had to 'fess up when Mom nearly had a heart attack after
reading the temperature of my light bulb—108.5°—and
momentarily thought she'd have to call an ambulance for
me. *Stupid lightbulb.*

I'd gotten a pretty bad burn on my index finger—a
blister had appeared there!—and a good talking-to. My

already frazzled mother ended with my least favorite phrase: "I'm very disappointed in you, Lauren." Then, worse yet, "You're still going."

It went without saying that my mood wasn't the best. I'd tried another horse yesterday and it hadn't gone well at all.

The horse, a beautiful Quarter Horse/Arabian mix, was sweet, but there was no chemistry between us. She did everything I asked, but there weren't any sparks. She seemed bored with every exercise we did.

Kim tried to reassure me that I'd only tried three horses and there were two more great options available on Thursday at Jeffrey's.

"You have all summer," she'd told me.

Everyone kept saying that, but this summer felt so short! Every day was going by faster than I'd ever imagined. Even though school had just let out, I already felt like Canterwood was going to happen way earlier than I was ready.

There were so many things to do, and finding the right horse to take to school was the most important.

"You look nervous," Becca observed from the seat next to me. Her voice was low. "Don't worry about Charlotte. She's going to be busy with friends, and you'll be at the stable all day. You'll spend more time with Taylor, Brielle, and Ana—you'll hardly ever even see her."

I rifled through my metallic gray purse, looking for some gum but more than anything wishing I had a cup of chamomile tea to calm my jangly, knotted nerves.

"It's just . . . it's my last summer at home before I leave for Canterwood. I wish it could just be the two of us."

Becca tugged down her graphic black T-shirt with a white heart on the tiny front pocket. She looked as though she wished the same thing but didn't want to say so. "Just try and go into it acting friendly. If she acts like a brat, then at least you know you tried. I'll do my best to run interference, too, if I have to."

"Thanks." I smiled at her and squeezed her hand in a silent gesture of gratitude.

Mom slowed the SUV, pulling up to the airport entrance. Planes roared overhead and a jumbo jet flew over us, heading toward the landing strip. The Union airport was tiny so it wasn't very busy. It was easy to find a parking spot near the entrance.

We walked through the glass doors and waited for Charlotte's plane. Mom and Dad kept their eyes on the exit, waiting to see Her Majesty come out.

"Ohh, she'll be out any second," Mom said excitedly.

I stood back and stayed by Becca, where I felt safe and invisible. I shifted my purse from one shoulder to the next.

A shock of white-blond hair stood out among the rest of the passengers. Dad stepped forward eagerly.

"Charlotte!" Mom called, waving. "Over here!"

Charlotte wheeled a purple carry-on suitcase behind her. A pink-and-black Hello Kitty laptop bag was slung over her shoulder. I was furious with myself for liking it.

"Hi," she said, letting Dad grab her in a hug.

Mom kissed her cheek.

"Hi, guys," Charlotte said, addressing me and Becca.

"Hey," I said.

As usual, Charlotte looked like she'd just stepped off a film set, not a plane. Her thick blond hair—newly cut, I noticed—grazed her shoulders. It was straight but full of smooth, shining volume—like she'd just had it blown out. She looked *très chic* and sophisticated, as usual, in black leggings with matte black ballet flats dotted with silver studs and a pink ruffle top. Her blue eyes—same color as mine—stood out against a thin line of smoky gray eyeliner. Her innocent peachy blush matched her glossy lips.

She sure was pretty on the outside. Too bad she was

anything but under all of that perfect makeup and designer clothing.

"It's good to see you," Becca said, reaching out to hug her. I read the formal tone in Becca's voice but only because we were so close. No one seemed to blink an eye at Bec.

For some reason, it made me feel good. It was nice to know that *one* person saw through Charlotte's act.

Charlotte hugged her back, then I put an arm around my oldest sister, doing that awkward pat-on-the-back hug.

"I'm glad to be home," Charlotte said, super chipper.

"We're glad to *have* you home," Dad said. "Do you have anything in baggage claim?"

Charlotte nodded, so we headed to baggage claim and got her other suitcase.

The five of us left the speck-on-the-map airport, making the short drive back home. Mom went with Charlotte up to her room right away to help her get settled in. From my room, I could hear laughing while Charlotte told Mom all about school.

"You're going to be such a big help to Lauren this summer," I heard Mom say. "I know you'll be able to make the transition easier for her with tips on decorating her dorm room, living with a roommate, and being away from home—all of that."

Charlotte was silent for several seconds. From the safety of my room, I rolled my eyes.

"Sure, Mom," she said finally. "Oh! So did I tell you about my history professor?"

I tuned out Charlotte and Mom, pulling my laptop onto my bed and logging into my new Canterwood e-mail. I had four new messages! Each one had a huge attachment. I clicked on the first one and it was from my English teacher. He'd sent a summer reading list and several journal assignments.

Canterwood wasn't kidding about having high expectations from its students academically. Every e-mail had a PDF attachment with a long, detailed list of work that had to be completed before classes began. I printed out the assignments, using nearly half a pack of paper, and organized papers into separate folders, each of which I'd labeled for every class.

For a moment I sat still, anxiety taking hold of me. Question after question ran through my head and pounded against my temples.

What if I couldn't handle the work at Canterwood?

What if I wasn't smart enough to keep up?

What if Yates classes were just easy compared to Canterwood and I'd only thought I could do well?

What if . . . what if I failed?

The last question knocked the wind out of me. I made myself take a deep breath, which came out sharp. I hadn't even started yet and the pressure to excel already felt crushing. Especially since I had no idea who—or what—I was up against.

Back when I'd competed, I'd traveled the country to participate in every A-circuit show in my division, all while juggling straight As and getting up at four to practice. In Connecticut, I'd excelled academically—graduating in the top 3 percent of my class at Yates, a prep school known as one of the most challenging schools in the state. It was often compared to Choate in terms of its academic environment.

But I also hadn't been home and off the circuit for long. Did I make a mistake? I loved Briar Creek, Yates, my friends, and being home.

Suddenly, I began to question all of my decisions. Question marks flurried around me like snow during a blizzard. I could barely see one day into the future.

Think about why you're going, I told myself. True, I *could* stay here and stay comfortable. I'd continue dating Taylor, riding Cricket at Briar Creek, hanging out with Brielle and Ana, and enjoying my popularity at Yates. Or, at least, I *had* been popular at Yates until I'd applied to Canterwood. If I did that, I wouldn't grow. I'd become complacent.

I *had* to take this chance. I'd regret it for certain if I didn't even try. Maybe I would flop at Canterwood. But if I didn't go and find out for myself, I'd be failing myself now.

I pulled my hair back into a messy half bun and got off my bed.

It was time for a cup of jasmine green tea, and then I'd be ready to attack the brand new pile of homework from Canterwood Crest.

Twenty minutes later my phone buzzed.

I took one more sip of my tea, put down my mug— another blue one, this time with dragonflies—and grabbed my phone off my nightstand.

There was a new BBM.

Taylor:

How's it going?

I smiled the way I did every time I saw his name.

Lauren:

Ok. Char just got home. We're staying out of each other's way . . .

Taylor:

Sorry. But @ least u'll be trying out more horses 2mrw and hopefully out w me on Fri?

Lauren:

I've been thinking abt Fri a lot. I'm excited 2 go out! ☺

Taylor:

Me 2. It feels like I haven't seen u in 4ever.

Lauren:

Same. Know what u want 2 do yet?

Taylor:

Dinner & night-walk in the park?

Lauren:

Wow—sounds perfect.

We chatted for a few more minutes. Once I finished my tea, I told Taylor I had to go start some homework for Canterwood. As I started math, my *best* subject, I couldn't stop thinking about Friday. Taylor and I definitely needed some alone time.

And it was time for us to talk and figure out where we were going.

I opened the red folder I'd labeled for math and pulled out a pen and a fresh spiral notebook. After I completed the first problem, I fell into a rhythm. The homework kept me from thinking too much about Charlotte, Canterwood, horses, or anything else.

At least in math homework, they were all problems I could solve.

23

A WELL-KEPT SECRET

DAD PULLED THE SUV TO A HALT IN WILDEN
Farm's puddle-filled parking lot. The sky couldn't have
been any darker or thunder any louder.

It had been pouring since late last night. Usually
I loved the rain. But today it felt like a bad omen. I
put down my phone, which I'd played with the entire
drive. I normally never did that when Dad drove me
somewhere.

"What's going on, sweetie?" Dad asked. His eyes
searched my face, looking concerned.

"Nothing," I said, pulling up the hood of my raincoat.
"Let's go."

"Lauren." Dad reached over and put a hand on my arm.
"Talk to me."

I sighed. The question had been nagging at me all morning, but I hadn't been able to say it out loud.

"What if these horses aren't right, either?" I asked. "What if we look all summer and never find the right one?"

Dad unbuckled his seat belt and turned slightly so he could look at me better. "If today doesn't work out," he said, "we're going to keep looking. Kim already has more horses lined up for you to try this weekend. I know how scary this is. But you've only ridden three so far, Laur-Bell. I know it can feel discouraging, but it's too early to give up. I'm going to take you to every farm in the area until we find *the* horse for you."

I smiled. Dad could always make me feel infinitely better.

"You won't go to Canterwood without a horse of your own," he added. "Remember: getting in was the hardest part—and you already did that! Now all that's left to do is the fun part! Picking out a horse, shopping for your dorm room—all that stuff is the part you're supposed to enjoy! Have fun with this part. It'll be over before you know it. Now, let's go take a look at what Kim and Jeffrey chose for you to try today."

"I'm ready," I smiled. And I was.

We got out of the car, hurrying through the rain and dodging puddles as we went. When got inside, I pulled back my hood and shook off my sleeves. I'd put my helmet in a protector bag so it wouldn't get wet.

"Hi, Gregg. Lauren," Jeffrey said, stepping away from one of the stalls. He had a clipboard in hand. "Right on time! I just finished taking inventory on the hay supply."

A door slammed in the parking lot and I watched as poor Kim ran through the rain holding a half-broken umbrella. A different groom came over and offered to take our raincoats and umbrellas. We all gladly handed them over.

"I'm sorry, Lauren," Jeffrey said. "But one of the horses I'd intended for you to ride today came up lame this morning. The vet checked him out and he'll be fine in a couple of weeks, but I'm afraid he's not in any shape for you to try him out."

"Oh, I'm sorry for your horse," I said, empathy coming through my veins. I hated when animals got hurt. "I'm glad to hear that he's going to be okay."

I'd known that *something* was going to go wrong today. I just *knew* I wouldn't be leaving Wilden a horse owner. We passed the hot walker where one of Jeffrey's grooms had five horses hooked up to the mechanical arms walking in a circle.

"Tell us about the horse you do have for Lauren today," Kim said, addressing Jeffrey.

"She's a new one," Jeffrey said. "Just got her. She's a Thoroughbred and Dutch Warmblood mix."

"What's her name?" I asked.

"I haven't even had time to give her one yet," Jeffrey said. He opened the side entrance to the arena, letting Dad, Kim, and I walk in first.

I looked over and saw Bryan, the groom I'd met last time, holding a stunning gray mare. She was tall—probably sixteen hands—with a delicate face.

"Hi there," I said, my voice soft.

I held my hand out to her, unable to stop staring. Her coat was the lightest gray and her black muzzle had a pink and white snip. I'd shied away from grays for so long since Skylight and my accident, but there was something irresistible about this horse. Seeing her coat color didn't send me into automatic panic. I saw *her*.

"She's a sweetheart," Bryan said, smiling.

The mare reached her muzzle toward me, her chin whiskers tickling my palm. I giggled. Her gentle dark brown eyes and long, dark lashes looked gentle as could be. Her mane, thinned and flat against her neck, looked silky.

"How old is she?" I asked.

"Six," Jeffrey said. "I bought her at an auction a couple of weeks ago. Her previous owner didn't know much about her past—he didn't keep great records on *any* of his horses. But I liked the way she moved, so I bought her anyway. Not something I usually do, but there's something special about her."

The mare breathed gently into my hand and I moved it to rub her neck. Her coat was glossy under the arena lights and she tipped an ear toward me, seeming to listen to my every breath. My every movement.

"Have any of your riders tried her yet?" Dad asked, a hint of worry detectable in his voice. I wondered if he was thinking of my accident. "I want Lauren to know what to expect."

"Bryan's ridden her several times," Jeffrey said. "He hasn't had any problems."

All I wanted to do was get in the saddle. I could barely contain myself. The mare was sweet, gorgeous, friendly, and gentle.

I put on my helmet and Bryan handed me the reins.

Don't get too excited, I warned myself. I didn't want to get my hopes up—I hadn't even ridden her yet.

I mounted and sat deep in the saddle. The gray didn't

make even the tiniest of movements until I squeezed my legs against her sides. We crossed the arena at an even walk.

I angled her parallel to the wall.

Thunder rumbled overhead and her ears swiveled, but she didn't lose concentration for one second.

I asked her to trot and posted, even though her gait was smooth enough for me to sit. We changed directions and I began to test her. I asked her to halt, which she did—immediately. She stood until I told her to walk again. We went through a few circles and serpentines—her movements flowing and her body supple beneath me.

We went back along the wall. I sat to her trot for a few seconds, then asked her to canter. She changed gaits without hesitation—her canter even. I slowed her, then asked her to back up. She tucked her chin, backing in a straight-arrow line.

I halted her, patting her neck. "Good girl," I said.

Her neck arched at my touch, her long tail swishing.

If I was going to Canterwood and had plans to compete in dressage, I had to try at least a couple of complicated dressage exercises with her. Nothing that would be overwhelming for her with a new rider, but just enough to give me a feel of what she could do.

I asked her for a working trot, and she moved forward with energy. She stayed collected and supple, sustaining the movement. I moved her into a twenty-meter circle, and her body bent easily. We moved through the circle, and she kept the right spacing as if she'd done a hundred circles.

I eased her to free walk, which was straight and easy. I wondered if she had dressage training—she certainly seemed to know what she was doing.

A slow smile spread over my face. Every inch of my body started telling me that this was right.

She was my horse.

I'd found *my* horse!

"Dad." With tears in my eyes, I turned her toward Dad, Jeffrey, and Kim. They all grinned at me.

"I think we have a match," Kim said, patting the sweet mare's shoulder—my sweet mare's shoulder!

"Laur-Bell," Dad said, his tone teasing. "I can't tell—what do you think?"

I leaned down, wrapping arms around the gray's neck. "I think she's perfect."

Dad turned to Jeffrey and shook his hand heartily. They moved a few feet away to talk and Kim joined them, but I barely noticed.

I dismounted and looked at the gray. At my horse.

I wrapped my fingers up in her mane, giving her another hug.

She smelled sweet, like grain and hay. When I looked at her, I didn't feel as though I'd be in the arena alone. The mare nuzzled my ear, as if she were going whisper a secret to me.

"Whisper," I said, trying it out. The word was soft and pretty—just my style. "Whisper," I said softly into her ear like a secret. She flicked her ear toward me.

"You like that, huh?" I asked, scratching her cheek. I leaned down and pulled out my phone from the only place I had room—one of my boots.

I held the phone so it faced us backward and I put my face next to Whisper's. Before she could move, I pushed the photo button and a soft flash went off on the camera. I examined the picture. Whisper's black-tipped ears pointed forward and she seemed to have been gazing at my phone. I saved it.

24
PRETTY PERFECT

"OMIGOD! OMIGOD!" BRIELLE AND ANA screamed at the same time. I'd dialed them the first second I could.

"I KNOW!" I practically shouted.

Since I'd left Wilden Farm a couple of hours ago, I felt as though I'd consumed ten cups of green tea, one of the most caffeinated of all teas.

Dad had called Mom on the drive home to tell her the news and she'd met me at the door. I told her *everything* about Whisper.

I never wanted to stop talking about her.

"The name is beautiful," Mom said. "How did you come up with it?"

"I didn't even think before I said it," I said. "It was so

weird—it was just her name—the way my name is Lauren and Becca is Becca."

"Lauren!" Ana said, laughing. "Hello!"

"Sorry!" I pulled myself back to the phone conversation. "I can't stop thinking about her. I haven't even told Becca . . . or Charlotte yet. They're still out."

"They'll be so happy for you," Brielle said. "Even Charlotte will be nice to you about *that*—it's amazing news!"

"Maybe you're right," I said, considering this. "I mean, it is a big deal. You guys—I have a horse! I can't wait for you to meet her. You're going to love her!"

"When does she come to Briar Creek?" Ana asked.

"Next week," I squealed. "We have all summer to get to know each other."

The thought was as comforting as a hot mug of Sugar Cookie Sleigh Ride tea. The next couple of months would give us time to get to know each other and practice together before we both went off to Canterwood.

I heard the front door close and then footsteps on the stairs.

"I've got to go," I told my besties. "But I'll talk to you guys later—promise."

Once we all hung up, I left my room and met Becca and Charlotte in the hallway.

"Hey, do you guys have a sec?" I asked.

Charlotte looked up from her phone screen. "*What*? I was just about to call Kieran."

Becca grinned. "What's up? It's big—I can tell."

"I tried another horse today," I said, focusing my eyes on Becca. "And guess what? She was perfect! I have a *horse*!"

"No. Way!" Becca hopped up and down. "*Lauren*!"

"I named her Whisper. She's gray and beautiful and the sweetest horse I've ever met," I said, barely pausing for air.

"I want to meet her!" Becca yelped. "This is *so* cool." Becca's gaze shifted to Charlotte. "Isn't that great, Char?"

Charlotte took a breath. "That *is* great," she said, finally. "I'm glad you got a horse, Lauren."

She gave me a half-smile and went into her room. Becca hugged me, smelling like she'd been trying a dozen body sprays at the mall.

"Did you take a body spray bath at Bath & Body Works?" I teased.

Becca let go of me and stuck out her tongue. "Ha. But seriously, I'm really excited for you. You know I don't know anything about horses so I don't know the right stuff to ask. The only thing I *do* know is that you know a good horse. I bet Whisper is pretty perfect."

"She is," I said. I felt like I'd fallen in love for the first time today. "She definitely is."

25
FINALLY READY

TAYLOR SLIPPED HIS HAND INTO MINE AS WE walked down the sidewalk.

We'd left the Italian restaurant a few minutes ago and had already walked the short distance to the park. Over dinner, I'd told Tay all about Whisper.

He'd been a good sport, smiling the entire time. He probably would've let me talk about her all night.

"I love seeing you so happy, Laur," Taylor said. "Whisper sounds like your perfect match."

"You should come with me some time to Briar Creek. I'd love for you to meet her," I said.

Taylor's easy smile was visible in the streetlight. The sun had set under half an hour ago and fireflies already dotted the grassy park.

We walked at an easy pace, neither of us wanting to be the bad guy and start the conversation. If I didn't just do it, I knew we might just lap the park until the sun rose again and my mom came to get us.

When we reached a park bench, I motioned to it. "Want to sit?" I asked.

"Sure," said Tay, obviously reluctant.

We sat next to each other, and I smoothed my jean skirt over my legs. I took a breath, trying to gather my thoughts, but I wasn't even sure how to start.

"I know you wanted to talk at the dance," I said. "But then I freaked because I thought you were going to break up with me."

"Laur—"

I touched his hand, stopping him. "I have to just get this out," I said. "Please."

Taylor nodded, his gaze settling on my face.

"I was scared. Of losing you, going away, missing my family, my friends. I wanted to enjoy that last night at Yates. I couldn't handle having this conversation with you because I wasn't ready for it then."

I looked down at my lap, then back at him. "I like you so much, Tay. I know you care about me, too."

"A lot," Taylor said.

I nodded, knowing I should let him talk, too.

"I was nervous at the dance, too," he said. "Because I was afraid that *you* were going to break up with me."

"Oh, Taylor," I said, shaking my head. "I didn't know you felt that way! I knew something was going on, but I thought it was because you . . . well, that you didn't want a long-distance girlfriend."

The street lamp above us caught Taylor's eyes—I could see the brilliant green even in the dark.

"That wasn't it at all. I'm sorry you thought that," he said. "Maybe I should have talked to you instead of trying to have a serious conversation like this at a dance."

"I'm sorry, too. I wish I'd done things differently. I wish I'd told you how I'd felt sooner, too."

We looked at each other, both falling short and silent. The noises of the park at night—dogs in the distance, crickets, frogs in the nearby pond—seemed unusually loud.

"What do *you* want?" Taylor asked, his tone gentle. The question was more inquisitive than combative.

I looked at him. Taylor Frost. My first boyfriend, whom I'd dated for five whole months. My boyfriend who smelled like chlorine all the time—not just after swim practice. Who could eat burgers every day and never get sick of them. Who listened to me talk about every riding lesson like it was the most fascinating thing he'd ever heard.

"I want what's best for you, for me, and for *us*," I said. I swallowed, knowing what I had to say but really, really didn't want to. "I think . . . I think that maybe what's best for us is if we stop dating. I care about you enough to say that, no matter how much I might prefer to stay together, just pretending that it will all be fine."

I watched Taylor carefully, but his expression was unreadable.

"I'm trying really hard not to be selfish. I want you to have a girlfriend that you can see—and hold hands with—every day if you want to."

I stopped and waited, not sure how he was going to react.

Taylor took my hand. "You're so amazing—you don't even know. I care about you, too. Thinking about you with another guy is . . . *really* hard. But I want all that stuff for you, too. It's not fair for you to be all the way over at Canterwood stuck with a boyfriend who lives hours away. Canterwood should be a complete and total fresh start for you, Lauren."

I sniffled. "This kind of sucks."

"I know." Taylor's chest rose as he took a deep breath.

"If I'd stayed at Yates, we wouldn't be breaking up," I said. "I ask myself a million times a day if I'm making the right decision leaving this place."

"It would be a mistake not to go," Taylor said. "This is the chance you've been working for, Laur! The shot that you've deserved ever since you first started riding. You're doing the bravest—the hardest—thing by leaving. I don't think anyone else in our class is as strong as you."

"Strong?" I asked. "Do you know how *scared* I am about all of this?"

"You wouldn't be Lauren Towers if you'd decided to do something just because it was easy. You'd be a cocky girl who'd get to Canterwood and mess it all up because she assumed she had the *right* to be there. But you see this opportunity for what it *really* is—a privilege."

"But this is a decision that affects everyone in my life—you, my friends, my family. I'm leaving *everything*. And maybe even being a little bit selfish."

"To do something amazing with your life," Taylor said. "Not to hurt people. I hate that you're leaving, but I'd be devastated for you if you hadn't gotten in. This, right now, is hard. But if we hadn't done this, we would have stayed together and both just been unhappy."

"I *never* wanted to break up with you," I said. "But I know it's right. How could we be together while we're really apart?"

I could see the pain in Taylor's eyes, but it was mixed with understanding and relief. I knew my expression was similar.

"I don't want you totally out of my life," I whispered. "I know I'm asking a lot, but could we still be friends? Somehow?"

Taylor squeezed my hand. "The only way I could handle you leaving is if we stay friends. I want to BBM you about swim practice and I want you to tell me what school's like."

I couldn't stop my eyes from getting teary. "I want that, too. Too many things are changing for us not to have each other."

We let go of each others' hands and Taylor wrapped his arms around me. I leaned into him, holding on. With each passing second, I felt like I could breathe a little easier, something I hoped would continue as I got closer and closer to Canterwood.

I still had time to get ready.

There was time to figure out how to be friends with Taylor. Brielle, Ana, and I would fit it a dozen or more sleepovers.

Becca and I would spend countless summer afternoons lounging in the pool.

Dad and I would drive to Briar Creek every day.

Mom would be there to help me pick out dorm room furniture.

Charlotte and I might even find something to bond over.

There were hundreds of mugs of kettle tea to find comfort—and home—in.

And Whisper. I had all summer to get to know my new horse—the one who'd be going along with me on this wonderful, terrifying journey.

For the first time since I'd been chosen, I felt like I was ready.

It was time to stop making so many lists. Choose to live *off* the paper more than coming up with ideas about how to live . . . in *theory*.

This wasn't just the end of a book—it was the beginning of a whole new series.

And I, Lauren Towers, would be the new main character.

ABOUT THE AUTHOR

Twenty-four year old Jessica Burkhart (a.k.a. Jess Ashley) writes from Brooklyn, NY. She's obsessed with sparkly things, lip gloss, and TV. She loves hanging with her bestie, reading, and shopping for all things Hello Kitty. Visit her online at www.jessicaburkhart.com.